Dreamer's Hideaway

Dreamer's Hideaway

The Widow's Watch
~ Book 2 ~

Mark E. Welch

CONTENTS

CHAPTER 1
Gaea

Gaea Pender raced across the front lawn toward her mother, her chestnut brown hair flowing in the summer breeze. Her powder blue dress danced as she flew into Cathy's arms. "Mom!" She cried happily. "I missed you!" Cathy dropped her purse and accepted her daughter's embrace, nearly falling backward to the ground. "I missed you too!" Her mother said, kissing her cheek.

Bill stood on the porch and smiled. He had plenty to smile about, he mused. It had been over eleven years since he bought the Shaw Estate. It had taken the following year to renovate the old manor; having had to gut it to the studs that held the structure up. The results were magnificent. He and Cathy had chosen not to restore the entire house. It would have been costly, and too many of the antiquities had been destroyed and proved to be impossible to replace. They upgraded the bathrooms, pantry, and kitchen to a modern style. They replaced most of the wallpaper with paint. In contrast, they replaced the flooring with the same native oak that had rotted away. Cathy absolutely would not budge to restore the grand staircase. "It is the focal point of the home." She would argue. Bill gave in rather quickly and was happy he did. The new stairs were equal to the original in their splendor.

For the most part, Cathy made the decisions for the décor. Bill thought about colors, fabrics, appliances; everything, including the kitchen sink. However, he was happy to sit back, watch the transformation, and continue his writing. Bill had two bestselling novels since the "Emissary's" success. The resurgence of his first novel, *The Dream Catcher*, and the addition of his latest: *The Spy Within Us.* Additionally, the "Emissary" movie had grossed millions of dollars worldwide. The stars were aligning with *The Dream Catcher* in production at Global Pictures.

Cathy approached her husband. "How was your day?" She asked, kissing him.

"Good. I picked Gaea up from school. She had her piano lesson, and I am nearly finishing the novel." He replied.

"Great! Can you put the Rover in the garage? I don't plan to go out again tonight." Cathy asked.

"Sure thing," Bill said, taking her keys and walking toward the SUV.

"Oh, and Bill?"

"Yeah, babe?"

"There are a couple of bags in the back. Bring them in?" She asked.

"Of course," Bill answered.

The original carriage house was beyond saving, so Bill had it demolished and, in its place, had a five-car garage built along with a second-story apartment. He reasoned that after Tracy's unfortunate death, guests might not feel comfortable staying in the main house. He had decided to add the apartment during the renovation and now considered it might have been overkill as the main house was quiet and new. When Gaea was born, Bill reconsidered his thinking and was quite pleased with the addition of the apartment. One day, she would become a young adult and head off to college. During the summer, she might want to come home, and if so, having her own space might prove to be beneficial, not only to his daughter but to him and Cathy as well.

Bill eased the Range Rover into the garage next to his Ford. The pickup truck had served him well. It was what he had taken Cathy out in on the night he proposed to her at the Cliff House. Now it was showing rust from the Maine winters and living on the coast of the

Atlantic Ocean. Salt and sand were not doing the truck any favors. His wife had begged him to trade it for a new model, but nostalgia kept the author in check. Cathy was on her third SUV. The Land Rover had become a Range Rover as she had insisted on a similar vehicle. Bill always caved into his wife's wishes. They had money, but she was a stickler on the budget, especially when Gaea came into their lives. He turned the SUV off and climbed out.

Cathy let go of Gaea's hand, and the girl ran straight to the piano. The old Steinway had not been savable, so Cathy opted for a new Yamaha grand piano to replace the old musical instrument. Gaea shooed Chimer off from the bench and sat down. Since the bonnet was kept up, Chimer had been relegated to lay on the piano's seat. The old cat yawned, climbed down, and stretched before wandering off and up the grand stairs.

"Look what I learned, mommy!" Gaea exclaimed and began to play "The Entertainer." Cathy could not help but be impressed by her daughter's musical talent as she listened. Gaea's music teacher had told her and Bill that she had a natural talent that was extraordinary. Talent that might call for a school such as Berkley College of Music or Julliard, she had said. Cathy walked to the piano and sat next to her daughter.

Bill opened the hatchback of the Rover and was greeted with the sight of six large bags. "A couple of bags, my rear end." He grumbled. He glanced into one and saw what appeared to be wrapped presents. "Shit." He said aloud. It was his daughter's birthday on Saturday. "Bill, you dumb ass." He had been so engrossed in trying to finish his novel that buying his daughter a birthday present had completely slipped his mind. He gathered up the bags clumsily and headed for the house. As he entered, Gaea was finishing with her impromptu solo. Bill dropped the bags in the foyer with a grunt. His wife stood up and ran over to him. "Bill, there is a cake in one of those bags!" She whispered, scolding him.

"I'm sorry, I just didn't expect to find half of Macy's in the back of your car." He replied grinning.

"Take them up to the bedroom," Cathy said.

"Yes, Ma'am. Um, honey?" Bill stammered.

"You forgot again, didn't you?" His wife asked, rolling her eyes.

"Well…"

Cathy sighed and said, "I bought it for both of us, so you don't have to worry. You always seem to forget your own birthday, let alone our daughter's. If you ever forget mine, you will be in a guest room for a month."

Bill smiled weakly. "I thought I married a kind woman." Cathy kissed her husband and hugged him. "You did, and I love you. Now take these bags upstairs—except for the cake. I will take care of that."

"Mommy?" Gaea called from in the great room.

"Yes, honey?" Cathy answered, returning to her daughter's side.

"Dad forgot my birthday again, didn't he?"

Cathy put her arms around her daughter and hugged her. "No. He would never forget that."

Gaea looked up at her mother and frowned. "I am not a kid anymore. It's OK. He always makes up for it. He's busy!" She shrugged in understanding.

Bill had paused at the landing and listened to his daughter and wife talking. "You idiot, you're real busy, Bill," he muttered to himself.

CHAPTER 2
Decorations

"You're kidding!" Denise squealed. "You want me to take the artifacts to the museum and work with Dr. Bastien to identify them? No Way!"

"Way," Cathy answered. "I need this done, but I don't have time to do it myself. He has agreed to help, so you go."

"He is so cute!" Denise exclaimed. "I remember when he came into the museum for the interview."

"This is a business, young lady." Cathy scolded. I am sending you to perform a task and not on a date. Understand?"

Denise composed herself and said, "Of course. I will always act professionally. You can count on me."

"You have been studying for this sort of thing."

"I have, and if it weren't for you, I would never have gotten this far," Denise said quietly.

"Take the items and get it done. I am confident that if you put your heads together, you can do the job."

"I will."

'Oh, and Denise?"

"Yes, Ma'am?"

"When you're done and off the clock…well, you know," Cathy said, smiling. "And one more thing."

"Yes, Dr. P?"

"That Egyptian piece, the one of Anubis. I think it is a fake, but I like it, and if it is not an original, I want it for my home library. Let me know, okay?"

"You got it! This is so exciting!" Denise giggled and ran off to collect the items.

Cathy rubbed her arm where she had been scratched by who she thought had been her cat, Chimer, years before. An attic was scary enough without having a cat come out of nowhere and rip its claws across one's skin. She still swore that the cat that attacked her was not Chimer. There had been no such odd occurrence since the restoration of the Shaw Manor, so Cathy simply brushed it aside. She gathered her purse and briefcase and left the shop.

Bill was busy with party decorations the following day, and he was lousy at it. He never could figure out how to tie a balloon after blowing it up, and most times, it got loose and screamed, flying in circles as it spun around the room. He did a few, then became frustrated and drove to the grocery store and had them give him a few dozen. Helium is better than air, he surmised once back at home and placing them in the formal dining room. Plus, the custom "Happy Birthday" balloons added an extra touch. The dining room was a wonderful choice for the party. Bill could decorate and then lock the doors so it would remain a secret until Gaea's friends arrived for the party.

He hung the balloons from the chandeliers over the new paintings that adorned the walls and let a half-dozen of them drift up to the ceiling. Bill laughed inwardly and walked out of the room. Pausing, he turned and peeked back long enough to turn out the light and close the door.

Cathy had done an amazing job. Her new shop was a boon when it came to redecorating the house. In Bill's opinion, the Shaw Manor had never looked better. It still held its former charm thanks to the ability of his wife, Cathy. She had been adamant that what was restored of the stately manor remain true to its previous owners' tastes and the Victorian Era style of the 1800s from which the now deceased Captain Shaw had chosen.

They had agreed on a major renovation to the second story except for the master bedroom. The five existing bedrooms were overly large and dividing them in half seemed wise. After demolition, reframing, plumbing, and electrical work, the manor had been converted into an eleven-bedroom, seven-bath. Eight bathrooms, considering the one that was added off the kitchen on the first floor.

From the start of the renovation/restoration, Cathy had been stern, and Bill had not been allowed to choose one item during the process, except for items for his new office in the widow's watch. He had claimed the one room as his so-called "Dreamer's Hideaway," where he could have his peace and write, surrounded by things that inspired him. Cathy had put up a half-hearted fight when he told her he wanted the tower for his office. He argued the need for an airy space that was quiet and inspiring. She noted his cravings for coffee and the long trek to the kitchen. His counter to place a water dispenser and a coffee maker in the widow's watch had closed the argument quickly. Bill's agreement to her leaving the museum and opening her own antiquities shop sealed the deal. He did have second thoughts about the arrival of their daughter, Gaea. Running up and down stairs to change diapers and feed a newborn would be a challenge. Cathy had simply laughed and reminded him, "It was your choice."

Bill turned the old skeleton key and locked the door to the dining room. He walked toward the washroom and saw Chimer eating from his bowl.

Bill tapped his forehead with the key and smiled. "Glad you're out here." He said to the cat. "Locking you in there would not have been a good idea." He entered the washroom and opened the key box that hung over the new front-load washer and dryer. He hung it up on an empty nail. Gaea was extremely smart for her age but not very tall.

"William E. Coyote…you're a genius," Bill said, closing the box with a chuckle. It was still early, so he headed to the widow's watch and his writing.

Gaea ran over to a table where her best friend Victoria was working on a project. Fourth grade had been a breeze for Gaea and now it seemed that fifth would not be any more challenging. Her teacher, Bessie Adams, had taken notice. More than once, Mrs. Adams had approached Gaea's parents suggesting that the girl take the Identified Education Needs test. Such a test, the teacher believed, could allow Gaea to skip a grade or maybe two or three. Bill and Cathy had declined. They believed in not only intelligence learned through teaching but also the value of experience gained through interaction with children of Gaea's age. Bessie Adams disagreed, but Gaea was not her child.

"What are you working on?" Gaea asked, twirling one of her long locks of hair around her finger.

"It's math," Victoria answered. "I hate this. These study sessions are horrible."

"You will get it," Gaea replied, picking up a pencil and chewing on the eraser. "They are doing these so that we can help each other. Please just try."

"I'm sorry. I will. Sometimes these sessions seem like I am back in baby school. You are just so much smarter than me."

"No, I am not." Gaea quickly refuted. "Hey! Are you coming to my birthday party?"

"Of course! I think all the kids want to go. You are the most popular girl in school."

Gaea lowered her voice and whispered into her friend's ear. "Victoria, you are my best friend, so I would be happy if only you were to attend."

She dropped the pencil she was holding and wrapped her arms around Gaea's neck. "I love you so much!"

"I love you too. Now let me show you how to solve this."

Bessie Adams sat at her desk, watching the two girls, and smiled. Perhaps skipping a grade was not such a promising idea after all.

Denise placed the neatly packed boxes into the trunk of her Escort and climbed into the driver's seat. She started the car and turned on the radio. Static filled the interior. She fiddled with the knob for a moment. Frowning, she turned the radio off. She turned the heat to high and gave a silent prayer that it would work. A bone-chilling moment later, warm air began blowing from the vents. "Stupid." She mumbled and headed off to the museum.

This was the first time that her boss had sent her on such an important task. She had been doing identifications and appraisals but those had been at the shop under the watchful eye of Cathy. Granted, she was not doing this alone and was technically aiding Dr. Jean-Claude Bastien, but it was still at the behest of Cape Neddick Antiquities and without the supervision of Dr. Catherine Pender. Denise was excited. The opportunity to examine a piece of possible Egyptian origin, as well as an oil lamp from the gold rush days of the

1800's and a Persian rug, was incredible, and she was determined to prove herself to her very meticulous boss

CHAPTER 3
Discoveries & Visitors

Dr. Jeffery Tarpon, a maritime archaeologist working with a grant from the University of Massachusetts, was narrowing in on a new prospective target off the coast of Southern Maine. He had been engaged diligently with Dr. Roland Brambilla, a marine archeologist and shipwreck specialist from Istituto Superiore per la Conservazione ed il Restauro in Rome, Italy. The two shared a common goal: to find and map lost shipwrecks along the coastline of the State of Maine in the United States. A daunting task, as known wrecks totaled over seven hundred, and only a handful of them had never been located. The two scientists believed they were on the right track to discover, catalog, and research more of them, and a blip on their sonar was warning of a possible target.

"You better get up here, Roli." Dr. Tarpon's voice came over the Archaean Horizon's intercom.

Dr. Brambilla rolled over in his bunk and looked at the small clock that sat on a side table. 2:00 AM. He pressed a button on the box and replied, "This had better be good."

"It is. Just get up here. We have found something. And it is big."

Dr. Tarpon and Dr. Brambilla had been colleagues and friends for years. Working in the same scientific field, however, was one of the few similarities they shared. The two men were only two years apart with Roland Brambilla being the senior of the pair, but Jeff Tarpon had been more successful. The scientist and professor led the way when it came to marine archaeology, and Jeff's published findings backed his resume'. Yet, his first choice when it came to a project was nearly always Roli. Dr. Brambilla had a passion for thoroughness, which most professional scientists would consider over and above when it came to initial objective observations. What Jeff might simply dismiss; Roland might take a day to analyze. The two styles of scientific theory, when put into practice, made the duo formidable within their field.

The pair could be compared in stature to Stan Laurel and Oliver Hardy from the Vaudeville days of comedy. In this case only the size of the two men were similar. Jeffrey Tarpon was tall and slim with starch white hair, while Roland "Roli" Brambilla was heavy set with jet black hair. Both men were dead serious when it came to their chosen professions.

Five minutes later, a very disheveled and partially dressed Dr. Brambilla stumbled onto the research vessel Archaean Horizon's bridge. He grabbed a cup of hot coffee held out to him by a crew member and squinted at the monitor Dr. Tarpon stood over. He shook his hand from spilling the coffee and licked it off. "What have we got?"

"See this thin line here and the cross-hash marks here and here?" Tarpon indicated, pointing at the screen.

"It is something big. I believe we have a wreck." Brambilla set his cup down and stepped to the nearby table. Using his finger, he traced a line perpendicular to a pre-drawn line and then to an intersection point. Making a mental note, he picked up the research logbook of the expedition and then looked at the data compiled of currently known shipwrecks. "There is no wreck reported at these coordinates."

"An intern could have told you that, Roli."

"I know. I needed to check it myself. You know how I am, Jeff."

"I do."

"We better wake up the team and prepare to dive this AM. What's the depth?"

"I figured you had checked that as well," Jeff said with a laugh. "Sixty meters, give or take."

"We best send down the Aquabot and have a look. In the meantime, we can gear up divers and get them briefed on where we want to concentrate for the first dive. We have the rest of tonight to get ourselves up to speed on this and formulate a plan. And I am going to be a member of the dive team." Roli said with finality.

Jeff smiled and clapped his friend on his back. "I had no doubt about that. I would recommend we begin here." He said, pointing to one of the thick, blurry horizontal lines. "I believe that these markings could be the midship of the vessel."

"I agree." Dr. Brambilla answered. "Cargo could still be scattered around the belly of the ship. It could make identifying her easier."

"If it is a ship." Jeff Tarpon pointed out.

"If." Roli Brambilla echoed, scratching his chin.

Mid-morning came with poor news. A storm was building to the west and the window of opportunity was closing on the team. Aquabot had provided some promising footage and did confirm their suspicions. It was a wreck that appeared to be from the 1800's. Dr. Tarpon was convinced it was a fishing vessel. Dr. Brambilla was not so sure. "Jeff, how can you be sure that this is a fishing vessel? There is no conclusive evidence."

"Look here." Dr. Tarpon said, pointing to what appeared to be a half-buried rusting anchor.

"So, it's an anchor. Many of the ships from the 1800's had anchors of that style." Roli countered.

"Perhaps. But look closer."

Dr. Brambilla looked intently at the still photograph displayed on the monitor. Leaning forward, he said, "Well, I'll be damned. There is writing. It looks like a part of a name. Cons?"

"Look at this." Jeff Tarpon said, handing a book to his colleague.

"Ah. The Constance. A fishing boat lost in the hurricane of August 1873 under the command of Capt. Wilbur H. Shaw. All hands lost." Dr. Brambilla finished reading aloud. "Do you believe it's the Constance?"

"One way to find out. Let's go grab that anchor before this storm rolls in."

As Denise drove into the Wells Maine Library and Museum parking lot, Dr. Bastien waited for her with a hand dolly. She parked next to him and got out of her car.

"Bonjour, Mademoiselle Denise!" Dr. Bastien said, kissing her cheeks.

Denise blushed and stammered, "Hello. I have the items in the trunk."

"Well then. Let us take them inside, shall we?"

Denise unlocked the trunk and the two loaded the artifacts onto the hand-dolly and took them up to the museum's laboratory. As Denise looked around, she surmised that the museum had not changed much since she had left. Dr. Bastien had kept it how Cathy had organized it. The exception is his office. He had replaced the pictures of Egyptian artifacts that had hung on the walls with ones depicting Asian culture. He had kept the same desk and chairs, and even the filing cabinets were as before. "Not much change." She murmured.

"What's that?" Dr. Bastien asked. "Oh, yes. The museum. I quite liked Dr. Pender's organization of the spaces. I saw no need to change anything. Well, except for small personal things and an upgrade to the computer systems. I am sure she would approve."

"No doubt," Denise replied, opening the Persian rug box. She plucked it out, and together, they rolled it onto the table.

Dr. Bastien handed Denise a pair of gloves and a magnifying glass. "I take it you have examined this piece?" He asked.

"Just a little. I believe it is nomadic, dating to about the middle of the 16th century, maybe the Zand Dynasty. This one is wool and a rather small sample of their work. In its size, I mean."

"Of course. And it's worth?"

"Somewhat of a guess, but I think maybe three thousand dollars or so." Denise shrugged. "Just a guess."

"A very educated guess, I can tell. Exceptionally good, Denise." Dr. Bastien said. "I think you hit the nail on the head. We will have to date it scientifically to be sure, but even without the test, I believe you are very accurate on this. Excellent work."

Denise smiled broadly and fiddled with her hands in front of herself.

The pair then examined the oil lamp, and after finding the stamp, "Made in Taiwan," hidden in the base, it quickly found its way to the donation pile.

The Egyptian statue was the last artifact, and the two examined it well into the evening. There were no markings to date it, and the carving itself baffled even Dr. Bastien. He had never seen such a piece from any of the Egyptian periods. He believed it to be of Anubis of the Old Kingdom. However, it was not quite right. He retrieved a book, *Egyptian Sculptures of Gods: The Old Kingdom,* from his office. Both he and Denise could see the discrepancies between the samples pictured in the book, which had been authenticated by various reputable museums and scholars, and the sample that was before them. None of the pictures showed the God of the Dead with teeth, especially fangs, as this artifact did. The paint on this piece seemed too brilliant, almost too fresh for its age. And there was something just not quite correct about the ears. Denise pointed out the fact that they seemed to be too short.

"I think you are right again, Denise. The ears of this statue are too short compared to the authentic statues of Anubis. I believe what we have here is a fake."

"Dr. Pender thought so as well. She said if it were worthless, then she would like to have it for her own collection."

"I'm not certain it is completely worthless." Bastien said. "There have been numerous cultures that have adopted the god Anubis for their funeral practices as well as numerous other rituals, not all of which were of a pleasant nature."

"Like the occult?" She asked.

"Very possibly, yes. Any such possibilities would have to be researched to determine if this item had indeed been used for such a purpose. Maybe Dr. Pender wishes to pursue such a task. In any event, it is late, and it is time to say goodnight."

"Oh wow, it is late," Denise exclaimed, looking at her watch. "I need to get home."

She placed the sculpture back into its box and headed for the exit. "I'll get this and the rug back to Dr. Pender." She said over her shoulder.

"Wait. Don't you want help?" Bastien asked.

"I'm fine! I have to go. Talk later, OK?"

"Oui," Bastien replied.

As the door closed behind the girl, Bastien scratched the back of his neck. He hadn't had the chance to ask Denise out for coffee. "Well, maybe next time." He thought, turning off the lights.

Bill was deep in thought when the doorbell rang. "Dammit." He said aloud. He got up from his desk and started down the spiral staircase. Bill had argued intensely to keep the old iron stairs. Rusted as they were, he felt a strange kinship with them. They seemed not only to belong to the old house but to be a part of it in a unique way. It was almost as if they were a piece of the heart of the old manor. He couldn't even explain it to himself, let alone his wife, but he argued to keep them. He argued until she gave in. Thousands of dollars later and nearly four months of work, they looked like they had been made yesterday, not a century ago.

The doorbell rang again as he made his way down the grand staircase. He cursed under his breath and made a mental note to have the monitor installed in the widow's watch, a speaker, and a relay button to unlock the door. Bill stubbed his toe at the base of the stairs and yelped as he nearly tripped over Chimer. He hopped into the foyer, fumbled with the lock, opened the door, and shouted, "What?!"

"Well, hello to you too." Clarissa Drake, Bill's literary agent, said with a smile. Her husband, Doug, stood behind his wife and dropped two suitcases to the ground.

"Ah, the newlyweds. Well, don't just stand there, c'mon in." Bill said, holding the door and rubbing his throbbing toe. The couple walked through the foyer and into the great room. "By looking at the luggage, you came for an extended visit."

"A couple of weeks," Doug said, extending his hand. "If you will have us. Clarissa was craving for a trip to Maine. I must admit, it beats New York City all to hell. And we never did have anything resembling a honeymoon. You know, writer's whining about this and that."

Clarissa elbowed her husband and laughed. "Jonesing was more like it. You know how I love the northeast, Bill. Especially Maine. And as far as clients go, Doug; Bill Pender is the least maintenance client I have."

"I wasn't talking about your clients," Doug said, smiling broadly.

"Well, you know you are both welcome in our humble abode," Bill said, closing the door.

"Humble. Right." Doug whispered into his wife's ear. Clarissa answered with another sharp elbow to Doug's ribs.

"You know where the guest rooms are. Pick anyone, except for Gaea's of course. Make yourselves at home. There is a fully stocked liquor cabinet, and the fridge is full. I even restocked the wine rack a couple of days ago, so enjoy yourselves." Bill looked at his watch. "Egad, look at the time. I need to pick up my daughter soon."

"Where is the little princess?" Clarissa asked.

"At school. It's still spring semester and she is getting out soon. She is still too young to be let off at the curb by the bus without one of us being there. I just go pick her up. Easier. And her mother would be appalled by having her daughter wait alone." Bill said with a laugh.

"I can't wait to see her. We brought her a birthday present!"

Bill hung his head for a moment. Even his agent remembered his daughter's birthday. "Bill, you are pathetic." He thought to himself. He would have to atone for this oversight.

"How long will you be gone?" Doug asked.

"What?" Bill said, turning his attention to his guests. "Oh, not long. Maybe twenty minutes. Depends on the traffic."

"That's great. Doug and I will run to the Viking for fudge and ice cream while you are gone." Clarissa broke in.

"Sounds good," Bill replied. "Cathy should be home by then as well."

"It's so good to see you, Bill," Clarissa said. "Doug, run the bags upstairs and toss them in a room. We can sort them when we get back."

"You got it," Doug said, picking up the luggage.

"Doug, when you get back, park your car in the garage. Use the last bay to the left. We are expecting a storm tonight. There is no need to leave your car out in the rain, and we need the parking space in the front for birthday well-wishers." Bill instructed.

"No car this time. We are cabbing it."

"You can use my pick-up then as well. We'll work that out." Bill said. As he headed to get his keys, his cell phone rang. "Hello. Pender the poet speaking."

"Silly. You know good and well who this is." Cathy laughed.

"Hm. Let me think. Can I check my little black book quick?" Bill snickered.

"Go ahead. I bought new pillows for the couch."

"Ouch. How are you, babe? I was just about to leave to go pick up Gaea."

"I'm good, and don't bother. I'm almost to her school, so I will get her."

"Sounds great!" Bill said. "Oh, Clarissa and Doug are here to visit and for Gaea's party. Don't say a thing. Let them surprise her, OK?"

"How wonderful! My lips are sealed. See you all shortly! Love you!"

"Love you too, babe." Bill hung up the phone just as the couple were heading out the door.

"See ya in a bit!" Clarissa said.

"Hey, get a pound of almond nut fudge for Cathy," Bill said, tossing his truck keys to Doug. "Garage, second bay from the right. Cathy is picking up Gaea."

"Will do!" Doug answered back. "Might get a couple of pounds of assorted for the party."

"Super!" Bill replied.

Bill, Doug, Cathy, and Clarissa sat around the kitchen bar, sipping white wine and chatting. Gaea was scrunched up on the floor watching Looney Toons and stroking a very content Chimer.

"I can't believe that parents are up in arms over children watching the cartoons I grew up with," Doug said, looking at the cartoon. Bugs Bunny was dressed in a skirt and kissing Elmer Fudd on his lips.

"We laughed at this stuff every Saturday morning," Bill added.

"So, Bugs Bunny is gay or something?" Cathy asked.

"Maybe transgender?" Clarissa proposed.

"Who was to say Bugs was even male?" Bill asked, taking a sip of wine.

"What a great point," Doug said. "Where was it even implied that Bugs was a guy?"

"I just don't get it. It's a freaking cartoon." Doug reiterated. "So, what if that stupid coyote blows himself up? He lives. There is never any blood or guts. Nothing like what our kids are watching today, which is violence personified."

Cathy giggled. "I always did like watching that stupid dog getting his ass whooped by the overgrown rooster. What was his name?"

"Who, the dog?" Bill asked.

"The rooster, you fool," Cathy answered

"Oh, Frog horn legs or something like that," Clarissa said.

Bill laughed so hard he coughed up his drink of wine. "Fog...Foghorn Leghorn." He spat out.

They all laughed causing Gaea to look up from her cartoon. "Can you people hold it down? I happen to be watching a classic cartoon." The four of them broke out in laughter once again. A few minutes passed, and the cartoon ended.

"Come, Gaea, it's bedtime," Cathy said.

"That's all, Folks!" Doug said in his best Porky Pig.

"It's bedtime for us all," Cathy said with a laugh. "I'm getting a little tipsy. And we have a special occasion tomorrow." Just then, lightning filled the windows, followed quickly by a low rumble of thunder.

"Storm is moving in, just like you said, Bill," Doug said.

"I'll pick up down here. You all head up." Bill said, starting to collect the glasses. The four stood up, and Clarissa and Doug headed for the grand staircase.

"I'll help, Bill." Cathy offered.

"Sure, babe. Thanks."

"It's so nice to be here," Clarissa told her husband as they started up the stairs.

"It's very cool to be back," Doug said. "It seems different. Very homey."

"The incident. Right?" She asked. Doug looked at his wife in acknowledgment. Gaea sped past the two, turning on the landing before running up to the second story. "Good night, Mom!" She yelled, disappearing down the hallway.

"I'll be up in a minute to say goodnight," Cathy called back.

"OK."

"It's nice that they showed up for Gaea's birthday," Cathy said, picking up a dishcloth. "Gaea will have all her friends here, but now we will have a couple of adults to help out."

Bill smiled, rinsing one of the glasses in the sink and handing it to his wife. "You mean helping control the chaos tomorrow?"

"Stop that. Just wait until you see the dress that I bought our daughter for her tenth birthday."

"I can't wait to see it," Bill replied. "I just hope that the balloons in the dining room will still have air by tomorrow."

Cathy kissed her husband and said, "Let's go to bed."

CHAPTER 4
A Statue and a Side of Pepper

Pepper & Pepper Publishing was booming not only due to best-selling author Bill Pender, but his success had become a magnet for other successful writers. Currently, the publisher represented and printed over eight of the top writers in the world, and Robert F. Pepper was elated. His demeanor in the office had not gone unnoticed by his staff, nor did it go unrewarded by their boss. Bonuses had returned to the employees of the publishing company, as well as raises and promotions. With the company's success came benefits to the people who made it all happen. Jack was one of the beneficiaries.

Jack Jefferson had joined the publishing firm just after graduating high school. He was what his classmates would have considered to be a nerd. A skinny boy with wiry red hair, a lack of athletic skill, and an acne magnet, or so the girls would say. The boy did have two very unnoticed talents. He could create a maze on paper that was nearly indecipherable, and he could write fiction. Unbeknownst to his student peers, Jack had published three short stories in obscure publications before he was a sophomore. He loved science fiction and horror, and the genre of the two seemed to dominate his writing. He had yet to summon up the courage to approach his boss on considering his recent novel for print. That all changed when Bill Pender became the hero for Pepper & Pepper Publishing. Robert Pepper had miraculously grown wings and a halo overnight. And the change gave Jack the opportunity he needed.

Bob Pepper had chosen to eat in the staff lunchroom, something he had never done prior to his company's current success. He had preferred to take his meals at his desk. After promoting three of his employees and giving all staff 3% raises, he upped it with a promise of Christmas bonuses returning this fiscal year. He found that he liked being around those who worked for him. He even increased his secretary's vacation time from two weeks to three paid. He seemed happy when young Jack Jefferson, arguably the hardest office worker he had, presented him with a 276-page manuscript for consideration.

"I'll take a look at this as soon as I can." Bob Pepper promised, setting the neatly typed stack of paper next to himself before digging back into his salad. Jack smiled broadly before excusing himself to return to his duties. Bob Pepper had also started making changes to better his health. "Dieting was the beginning," he told himself. He still could not bring himself to drop the cigars or his beloved Scotch.

The editor put the last page of Jefferson's manuscript down on his desk atop the rest of the loosely stacked pile. Reaching into his drawer, he pulled a brown legal legal-sized envelope from its depths. Carefully, he shuffled the manuscript back into a tidy pile and slid it into the envelope. He sealed it and wrote *EDITORIAL* neatly on it before adding his signature. Pepper sealed the envelope and, reaching into his desk, retrieved a rubber stamp. He pressed PRIORITY onto it and relit his cigar. "Dorothy?" Pepper said into his intercom.

"Yes Mr. Pepper?" His long-time personal secretary answered. "How can I help you?"

"I need to send a manuscript over to editing."

"I will have Jack Jefferson bring it straight over." She answered.

"No. Not Jefferson." Pepper said, puffing on his cigar. "Send someone else, OK?

"Yes, sir. Right away."

"Thank you," Pepper said and severed the connection. "When it rains, it pours." He thought. "Right under your very nose."

Denise was excited and nervous as she drove toward the Shaw Estate. She had gotten up especially early to deliver the statue to her boss Cathy. Today was special for the entire Pender family, as it was their daughter Gaea's birthday party. Denise had been invited, and she thought it would be great to bring her gift for Gaea and the fake statue of Anubis for Cathy. She turned the radio on, and music filled the car. "The radio works!" She said aloud and turned onto Shore Road.

Morning came, and four adults awoke to the happy shrieking of the birthday girl charging up and down the manor's second-story hallway. "Mom! Dad! Get up!" the young girl screamed happily. "It's my birthday!"

Bill groaned, rolled over, and poked his wife. "It's your turn." He said sleepily. Cathy sat up and laughed.

"What?" Bill said groggily.

"She doesn't need her diaper changed, silly. It's her birthday." Cathy said, whapping Bill with a pillow. "Now get up. We also have guests, and I need to start breakfast."

"And make coffee. Strong coffee." Bill moaned and buried his head back into his pillow.

Cathy jumped up and donned her robe. She checked herself in the bathroom mirror and, with a quick brush of the hair, headed out into the hallway and into the arms of her daughter. "Mom!" Gaea exclaimed.

"Good morning, Princess Gaea! Shall we retire to the kitchen and prepare breakfast?"

Gaea curtsied. "I believe we shall. There are famished mouths to feed."

"Famished? Such a big word," Cathy exclaimed, taking her daughter's hand.

"I read it in one of my books," Gaea replied. It means hungry, doesn't it?"

"It sure does, and right now, I am famished."

"Me too!"

Forty-five minutes later, the four adults plus one extremely excited girl were gathered around the breakfast table. Cathy had insisted on having a table that sat six near the kitchen so that there could be family time that was not so stuffy as eating in the formal dining room. Bill had been all for it, and after the pair spent time doing online shopping, they decided on a rustic and authentic shaker-style table and chair set that was made by the Amish. Cathy simply adored the natural finish on the oak that the craftsman had chosen. Bill had to admit that the piece was beyond his expectations. After all, he had told his wife that a simple folding card table would have done nicely.

"Cathy, this is perfect," Doug said, ripping into a piece of honey-baked ham. "And the pancakes are delish."

"I have to agree," Clarissa said, taking a sip of her tea. "How did you whip up ham so quickly?"

"We had it last week. Leftovers can be the best sometimes."

"Here, here!" Bill said, laughing. "Just wait until you try my three-day-old chili!"

"Mom, where are the donuts? We always have donuts." Gaea said, taking a drink of her milk.

"Not this morning. There will be cake later."

"But I wanted both," Gaea said, pouting.

The adults all laughed, and Bill pulled his daughter into him for a partial hug. "Cake is better, baby."

"Mom. Can I go to my room? I want to get ready."

"Of course. I'll go with you. I have something special for you." Her mother answered.

"What is it?" Gaea asked excitedly.

Cathy stood up. "Come on, you'll see."

"The dishes are up to me," Clarissa said, standing and picking up her plate.

"I need to check the dining room and see if the balloons survived the night," Bill said

"What can I do?" Doug asked, collecting dishes.

"Help me," Clarissa replied.

The doorbell rang as Bill took the dining room key from its hook.

Cheering ensued as the rusted anchor was laid gently on the research vessel Archaean Horizon's aft deck. The rain had begun to fall, and the wind was picking up. Men and women scrambled to secure the ship, including the Aquabot, which was currently being untethered and lowered into the bowels of the ship.

"We're going to have to get it below, Jeff." Doctor Brambilla said over the noise of the ship and the wind. "We can't examine it out here!"

"Yes!" Dr. Tarpon yelled back and waved to one of the attentive students who looked over the relic intently. "Get this below and into the lab. We need to secure it as soon as possible!"

"You got it!" The young man replied and quickly started to prepare for the move.

Two hours later, the captain of the Archaean Horizon had turned his ship into the wind. The anchor had been secured in the lab and the two scientists had conceded that any examination of their new find would have to wait until the storm passed. One could hardly walk, let alone do research in such a gale.

Bill opened the door to a smiling Denise VanDusen holding a rather large box. He had liked the young girl since the day he had met her. Her bubbly personality and a smile that would melt some lucky guy's heart, Bill thought. "Hey there!" He said reaching for the box. "You're early for the party. And what's in the box?"

"Hi! It's a statue that Dr. Pender, er, Cathy, wants for the house. And I was excited for Gaea's birthday party, so I thought I would come early and help set up."

"How thoughtful," Bill said setting the box down in the foyer. "I'll let Cathy deal with this. Come in."

"One sec. Let me get Gaea's present from my car."

"Sure. Just close the door behind you. I'll be in the dining room."

"Cool," Denise said and turned to run to her car.

"I hope Gaea likes our present," Doug said, placing a dish back into the cupboard.

"What young intelligent girl doesn't like a book? A rare book at that?" Clarissa replied washing a cup.

"It's the rare part I am concerned with. That copy of *Through the Looking-Glass* was expensive and exceptionally rare. I hope it eventually ends up in Bill's library until she is old enough to appreciate it." Doug said.

"I'm counting on it. Once Cathy sees the gift, she will take the proper actions."

"I hope so."

"We had better start gathering the paper plates, cups, and the rest of the stuff for the party and bring them to the dining room while Gaea is busy upstairs. Cathy said it's all in a bag in the washroom." Clarissa informed him, handing her husband the final spoon to wipe.

"OK. And why couldn't we have simply put this stuff in the dishwasher?" Doug whined jokingly.

"Don't be so lazy, Doug. There were only a couple of things. Besides, doing dishes gives us time to talk. C'mon, let's go get the party favors."

"It is lovely," Cathy said, admiring the statue now displayed at the treble end of the piano sitting on the floor. The artifact stood keyboard high and made a distinct endpiece for the grand piano.

"It is unique," Bill said turning his head to one side as if he were trying to create a perspective within his mind. "It's Egyptian, you say?"

"It looks strange," Clarissa said.

"It looks Egyptian," Doug added.

"It's scary," Gaea said from the bottom of the staircase. The girl looked adorable in her new pink dress. Her hair was done up in a bun, and her new blue shoes complemented the ensemble perfectly—all except her eyes. Normally bright and sparkling with inquisitiveness, they looked dark and ominous as she stared at the statue.

"Baby!" Her mother exclaimed running to her daughter's side. "It's just a piece of art."

"It's scary," Gaea said again.

"It just looks scary, honey," Bill said walking to Gaea's side. He crouched down and hugged her. "Mommy is right. It's just a statue. An old statue."

"And no, it is not Egyptian. It's a facsimile." Cathy remarked. "A fake."

Gaea stood and continued to stare at it.

CHAPTER 5
Vicky

People began to arrive shortly before noon, and Gaea insisted that she be at the door to greet them. "After all," the girl said, "They are my guests." Who was Bill to argue? He stood idly by watching as his daughter opened the door and greeted Mr. Jeff Walsh and his daughter, Victoria, with all the grace and tact of a well-trained butler.

"Victoria, darling. How nice of you to attend." Gaea said with a curtsey.

Victoria's curtsey equaled Gaea's, and she said, "Moi? Miss such an auspicious occasion? It would mean the death of me!"

"Come, my love. Let us retire to the great room." Gaea said, taking her friend's arm. After walking regally out of the room, the two charged off laughing and screeching loudly, leaving the two men staring after them. Turning, they faced one another and broke out laughing. The two girls paused in the kitchen before grabbing a chip from a plate.

"That was great!" Victoria said, giggling. "I thought my father was going to fall on his face. I would not even know that French word if not for you."

"Your dad? Did you see mine? And you're welcome."

"I wonder if they bought the act?" Victoria asked.

"Not for a second," Gaea answered. "But it was funny!"

"And what is all the noise about?" Cathy asked entering the kitchen from the washroom. "Do I behold two lovely ladies of the court?"

"Hi, Mom! Look who's here!" Gaea answered.

"Hello, Mrs. Pender," Victoria said shyly. "My dad is with Gaea's dad in the living room."

"Thank you, Victoria. I will go say hello. In the meantime, why don't you both go up to Gaea's room? It's still early, and I will call you both when the other guests arrive."

"Come, love. I have new dolls to show you." Gaea said taking her friend by the hand and heading for the back staircase.

Cathy watched as the two disappeared, skipping through the panty and washroom. She could hear the girls' shoes as they clacked on the narrow wood back stairs leading to the manor's second floor.

Bill led Jeff to the fireplace and motioned for him to sit down. He turned and walked to the wet bar that stood as an extension of the breakfast bar. Along with the faux wine cellar Cathy had constructed into the pantry, she also had a bar built, which had a fantastic view of the Atlantic. The bar was fully stocked with some of the finest bottles of various liquors available and had bottles of the Pender's favorite and select white wines. A double sink and an icemaker made the addition a bartender's dream.

"What can I get you?" Bill asked.

"Something light. Driving, remember?" Jeff said, staring into the fireplace. Flames licked at a dried piece of oak that Bill had placed upon smoldering embers. "It's been years since I've been in this old house."

"Really?" Bill asked. "I had no idea." Bill handed Jeff a beer bottle and sat in a chair that complemented the couch.

"Ayuh. It was a long time ago. Just me and a couple of other kids decided to go on an adventure to an old haunted house." Jeff said with a weak smile. "I don't remember it looking like this."

"We renovated it after I bought it," Bill said, sipping his ice water.

"I remember," Jeff said. "I had just married my wife, Barbara. She and your wife Cathy were never much of friends. With different interests in school, Cathy was a year older. You know that sort of thing. But I took notice. Mind you, not because of Cathy or the famous Bill Pender. I took notice because of this house."

"Where is your wife?" Bill asked, trying to change the subject.

"Dead," Jeff replied flatly. "She caught the cancer just after Vicky turned one."

"Ouch. I'm sorry."

Jeff looked up from the bottle of beer he held in his lap and smiled indifferently. "It came on quickly, and she was gone in less than a year. It was only me and Vicky when she turned two. And don't you go calling my daughter Vicky. She only answers to Victoria these days." Bill turned his head questioningly.

"Vicky was her mother's pet name for her. When she was old enough to talk and understand, start school and that sort of thing, she started demanding to be called Victoria. I just let in and did what she wanted. It's hard being a single parent with no schoolin' on how to raise a young one. If it wasn't for my own mother, God rest her soul; I don't think I'd have made it this far." Jeff wiped a quick tear from his eye and took a deep drink of beer emptying the bottle. He held it up, and Bill took it.

"Another?"

"Ayuh. I think I'll have one more." Jeff said, slouching back onto the couch. "I don't normally drink. I swore it off after I lost Barbara. I only touch it now at certain times." Jeff smiled broadly seeming to remember a fond memory. "I have one glass of champagne by myself on April 27th."

"Wedding day?" Bill asked softly standing up to get another beer.

"Nope," Jeff answered. "It was the day I asked Barbara to marry me. We took a walk up in Wells and out onto that jetty. The one that runs along the harbor. I'll never forget it. It was a full moon and she…my beautiful Barbara, she looked so beautiful. I just broke down and asked her. She said yes."

Bill sat down on the couch next to Jeff and handed him the bottle. "My God, Jeff."

"Well, it's a happy day today, right?" Jeff said taking a drink. "If it weren't for that daughter of yours my Victoria never would have learned those girl things that I could never teach her. I am incredibly grateful for that, Mr. Pender."

"Gaea considers Victoria her best friend," Bill remarked.

"Victoria has had trouble tryin' to fit in. Shy she was. I even tried to get her a pet, but she would have none of it. The first time she ever came home from school with a smile was when she met Gaea. I'll never forget how she just would not shut up about her new friend. How smart Gaea was. How beautiful Gaea was." Jeff smiled again, taking another swig of beer.

"The school has been after Cathy and me to give her a test that would let her skip a grade or two. It is some type of intelligence test." Bill said.

Jeff looked up alarmingly and said, "You wouldn't take Gaea away from…"

"Not a chance," Bill said with an assuring tone of voice. "We think that having her go through school, well, like you and I did, is important. All the experiences that kids go through when they are young. I could never take that away from Gaea." Bill momentarily thought, then added, "Just think of what the two did together. They tried to pull a prank on us! How can I ever even think of denying my daughter more times like that?"

"Bill, you are a very special man, and I hope to call you a friend."

Bill extended his hand. "Of course. Victoria is like family here now. Like a sister to Gaea. And she is welcome here anytime."

Jeff grabbed Bill's hand and then pulled him into a bear hug. "With a friend like you, Bill, I just might see my daughter through."

"Without a doubt, Jeff. Without a doubt."

Jeff stood up and looked at his watch. "Darn it, look at the time. I gotta go. I have a fill-in shift down at the high school. I'm a maintenance man. I'll be back in a few hours to pick up Victoria."

"Sure thing, Jeff," Bill said.

Jeff started to head for the door when Bill called after him. "Hey, Jeff? When was the last time you had time off?"

"It's been a spell," Jeff said, stopping at the front door.

"Tell you what," Bill said. "Give me a call in a couple of hours. If Victoria is having the time of her life with Gaea as I suspect they will, let her stay over. I'm sure the girls would love it."

Jeff considered for a moment. "Hm, it would be Victoria's first time away from home all night, but I think that would be fine. I will call later, OK?"

"You got it."

Bill watched Jeff drive away in his old Chevy pickup truck. He was about to close the door as another car drove up. By the looks of the pink balloons in the back of the SUV, it was clearly another party guest. Bill reopened the door and walked onto the porch to greet the new well-wishers.

"I don't like that thing by the piano," Gaea said, adjusting the dress on one of her dolls.

"Why?" Victoria asked.

"It looks at me funny."

Victoria laughed. "How can a statue look at you? You're silly."

Gaea shrugged and looked at her friend. "I don't know. I just feel weird when I'm near it."

"Don't go near it then."

"I have no choice because of my piano lessons."

"Oh," Victoria said.

"Do you like my dolls?"

"I love them. I only have one. My dad can't afford to buy me much." Victoria jumped up and ran to the bedroom window. "And you have such a great room. Mine is small."

Gaea walked over and stood by her friend. "I would like to see yours sometime."

"It's so much nicer here," Victoria said wistfully. "Just look at the ocean. It is so pretty. All I see from my window is a car and the woods."

"A car?"

"It was my mom's. When she died, my dad left it there, and now it's rusty. I hate looking at it."

"Here," Gaea said, pressing the doll into her friend's arms. Take her. I want you to take care of her. She was an orphan, and she did need a home and a mama. And I think you are a perfect mom for Sandy!"

Victoria grasped the doll and looked at Gaea. "But how can she be an orphan?"

"My mom brought her home from her shop. A doll in a shop with no one to care for her is an orphan. No mom or dad." Gaea said, stroking the doll's red hair.

"So, I am a half-orphan?" Victoria asked.

"No, you have your dad, and there is no such thing as a half-orphan. Plus, you have me, and now you have Sandy!" Gaea exclaimed pulling her friend into a fierce hug.

"Gaea?" Victoria asked drawing away from her friend. "Before, you know...when my mom died, she used to call me Vicky. She was the only one that called me that. Except, well, my dad tried, but I hated it."

"I love Vicky. It's so pretty. Why do you hate it so?"

"It made me sad. All I could think about was my mom." Victoria shrugged.

"Well, Vicky is a great name, and if your mom chose that for you, it has to be special!"

"You can call me Vicky from now on, Gaea," Victoria said quietly. "If you want to."

Gaea hugged her friend again. "I would love to! I just love the name, and it fits you perfectly."

"You are my best friend, Gaea."

"Gaea? Victoria? More of your friends are here." Cathy called. "Come downstairs."

"Coming, Mom!" Gaea shouted back, then whispered into her friend's ear. "Vicky."

CHAPTER 6
More Discoveries

"The site is going to be a mess." Dr. Brambilla said plopping down in a chair of one of the vessel's laboratories. He drank deeply from his mug of coffee and rubbed his neck. "That was some storm, and God knows how much of the wreckage has been strewn across the bottom."

"That it was." Dr. Tarpon said, jotting notes into a fresh notebook. "I, for one, hope that not much of it was disturbed. It's been lying there for decades and at a deep depth. But we can only rely on our equipment for now. The water might not be clear enough for static cameras and video for a couple of days."

"I guess we best spend some time on this hunk of iron then. Have you made out any more of the ship's name inscribed on it?"

"I'm afraid not. I think it's going to need to be cleaned," Jeff paused and then added, "and cleaned carefully."

"Acid bath?" Roli queried.

"I was thinking that, but it will have to be diluted. Otherwise…"

"Otherwise, we lose rust, metal, and the name."

"You bet. I think we go old-school archeology on this. Weak acid and soft brushes. A little at a time. We don't have the facilities here on the boat as we would back in our labs." Jeff stated.

"Agreed, my friend. We can have the understudies start on this task. You and I must jump back on deciphering the rest of that wreck." Roli Brambilla said, gulping down the rest of his coffee and handing the empty cup to an attentive intern. I, for one, want to know more about this Constance and Captain Wilbur H. Shaw, whoever he was. If, in fact, we have found his boat."

"Yes, Roli. Captain and crew can make up most of the ship's story." Jeff reflected before adding, "And the reason she was lost. Most boats do not just sink because of a storm."

"I do want to keep a close eye on this anchor, Jeffrey. We can't afford a slipup by a student destroying our only recovered artifact."

"By the book, then."

"By the book indeed." Dr. Brambilla said, taking a fresh cup of coffee from an understudy.

"What is it?"

"I think it's an ancient Egyptian statue." Diana Caron said to her friend Donna Hulsey. I am no expert, but I remember something about Egyptian demons that people worshipped."

"Not quite," Cathy said, approaching the two women. She handed them each a glass of white wine and smiled. "Are your kids having a good time?"

"The best," Donna said, sipping her glass.

"I am having the time of my life," Diana said. "I have wanted to see the inside of this manor for years. I always believed this house was simply an old, lost, and forgotten wreck. I can't believe what you and Bill have done to the place. Simply stunning."

"I agree. It is unbelievable. But this statue is quite different."

"Anubis," Cathy said, turning her attention to the statue. "And yes, it is quite interesting. And a fake."

"A fake?" Donna asked.

"Well, as Egyptian history goes, yes. But not totally a fake when it comes to religious artifacts."

The two women looked at each other and then looked back at the statue.

"Egyptians had both gods and demons. Demons in Ancient Egypt were supernatural creatures that mediated between gods and humankind. They are generally depicted as hybrid creatures with human bodies and animal heads. Even though Anubis has a man's body with a dog's head, he is not a demon. He was the god of mummification and the afterlife and the patron god of lost souls and the helpless. Not all gods were good, but they were all worshipped for what they represented. Our fake friend Anubis here was the God of Death and the protector of the underworld."

"Satan," Diana said.

"No." Cathy countered. "The underworld for the Egyptians was a place to be feared but a necessary path to traverse to get to the afterlife. It took a great deal to achieve the admittance to such an afterlife and the glory that awaited. Having great wealth, it seems could buy one in. Or so the pharaohs thought. Anubis was a key to making that journey for all ancient Egyptians."

"So, then, what is this?" Donna asked. "If it is not Anubis?"

"I only have a guess, but I think it is a depiction of an 18th-century demon that was worshiped by a group of men who were cast out from an organization called the Strange Fellowship. I have not been able to verify that, however, I do have a strong suspicion."

"Dr. Pender?" Denise asked. The girl stood behind the three women listening intently to her boss. "Do you really think that statue is a demon?"

"Of a demon," Cathy said, acknowledging her young employee. "I'm sorry. Denise, this is Donna and Diana. Ladies, my very astute young protégé. As I said, I believe this is a fake, or in this instance, a bastard statue of the god Anubis."

"I heard you say that, Dr. P." Denise giggled.

Cathy laughed and said, "I wouldn't worry. It's only a piece of mud that was baked in an oven and then painted. The Wicked Witch of the West would be more of a threat than this thing. It's art and nothing more. Besides, it's going up to the library where it belongs with the rest of my relics."

"You want me to bring it up there now?" Bill interjected, smiling broadly. "I think it is ugly as well, and Gaea seems to hate it."

Cathy sighed. "Like I said, it's going up to the library with the rest of the relics…just like my husband here."

Bill gave his wife a look, then a peck on the lips before scooping up the stature and heading for the grand staircase. The women laughed as he turned and left.

The house was filling quickly with children excited to attend Gaea's birthday party, as well as their parents, who were equally excited to be in the Shaw Manor and for the opportunity to hobnob with the famous Bill Pender.

The author had expected an onslaught of children, not a herd of adults invading his personal space and home. When the first request came for an autograph, Bill left the fiasco to his wife and retreated to the widow's watch and sanctuary. Having an office that was only accessible through the master bedroom had proven to be a boon. Not even the most obnoxious guest dared to violate the sanctity of a bedroom. It also helped that no one knew the whereabouts of his private office. Bill felt safe in his mancave.

He did, however, know he would have to make an appearance and do the dreaded mingling before his daughter's birthday party started. With the thought of the open bar, his heart sank further. The more alcohol that people drank, the more it could not be a good thing. The longer he could avoid the inevitable, the better.

Bill had chosen a rather poor place for the statue when he initially brought it to the widow's watch. He had moved it repeatedly, standing and looking at it from various angles, but no area of the office seemed to suffice. He finally placed it near the balcony next to a pot that held a half-dead ivy plant. Another relic that Cathy had decided to put in his office. She had told Bill to water the plant. He had not, and now as he looked at the statue next to the partially dead plant, he rather thought the two were paired quite nicely. The dead and the partially deceased. He moved one of the curtains that hung covering the windows over them. Bill smiled at his solution and closed the doors to the balcony as his wife called to him from the base of the spiral stairs.

"Coming," Bill called back.

Fred Black stood in front of the fireplace admiring the painting that hung over the mantle. Bill walked over to the bar, grabbed two beers, and joined his guest. He handed one to Fred and held his bottle up.

"Cheers," Bill said. "Bill Pender."

"Cheers," Fred answered. "Fred Black. I was just looking at this painting. The couple. Are they the Shaws?"

"They are. Cathy, my wife, had that done. It is one of two. The originals hang in the Cliff House. Cathy tried to buy them, but they were not for sale for any amount of money. So, she had pictures taken, sent them to New York, and painted replicas. The other is on the landing of the grand staircase."

"That is where I know this one from," Fred exclaimed. "I dine up at the Cliff House several times a year and always pause to admire the good captain and his wife. Handsome couple."

"That they were," Bill replied.

"And, by the looks of things, you and yours have done right by the manor. Quite lovely." Fred turned and faced Bill. "You are a very talented writer." He added.

"Thank you," Bill said nervously. "Was another autograph in the works?" He thought to himself.

The older man scratched his graying beard. "I was a well-read writer in my day. I came to hate the popularity that went with it. Just as I see how you are now, I once was. You are nervous. There is no need to be." Jack handed the bottle of beer, still full, to Bill.

"Fredrick Johansen Black?" Bill asked, setting the bottle on the table.

The man looked up at Bill and smiled. "Yes."

"I have one of your books upstairs in my library," Bill said. "I have read it, and I found it fascinating. Your knowledge of this state is incredible."

Fred sighed. "You have a passion, don't you, Bill?"

"For writing? I can't survive not getting the pictures out of my head and onto paper. Sometimes I feel like my brain will explode if I can't be by myself for a few hours in front of my computer."

"I felt that way. Still do." Fred said, smiling. "My mind is not quite as sharp as it used to be. I tend to forget things, and it is quite frustrating. I just turned ninety years old last month. Age does things to a person, or in my case, an incredibly old man."

Bill sat down and stared at Fred. For the life of himself, he could not see the years on the man. A day over sixty maybe. But nine decades was hard for Bill to grasp. "How many have you written?" He asked quietly.

"Oh," Fred answered, sitting on the sofa beside Bill. "Hundreds, if I were to take a guess. Maybe even thousands. Most were not published, mind you, and sit in my study stuffed into filing cabinets and boxes." Fred leaned towards Bill and chuckled. "I didn't have those fancy computers back then, so I used paper and a typewriter. Those machines use a ribbon."

Bill sat fascinated by the old man. Of all the people who could have shown up to his daughter's birthday party, Fred Black, a noted Maine writer, was sitting next to him and talking shop.

"Why are you here?" Bill asked.

"Oh yes. That would be my granddaughter, Alisha. Her mother, my daughter, is a single mom and works for the State of Maine. She has been pestering her mother to be able to attend your daughter's party. I guess that is how I got drafted when my daughter was called away." Fred winked at Bill and smiled. "And how could I refuse? A chance to meet *the* Bill Pender. The rising literary star? Not only you but this fabulous manor. It was an old author's dream come true."

"I am flattered, Fred," Bill replied.

"Don't worry, I won't ask for an autograph," Fred said slapping Bill on his shoulder.

"Grandpa!" A young girl yelped running up and jumping into Fred's arms.

"Alisha, my love. May I introduce you to one of the most popular novelists of our lifetime?"

"Hello, Mr. Pender." The young girl said politely.

Bill smiled at her. Alisha was adorable. Her black hair and equally dark eyes stood out in stark contrast to her perfect white teeth that were surrounded by her captivating smile. She wore a bright white dress that the powder blue laced trim accented perfectly. The girl's black shoes caught Bill's eye, reminding him of a pair he had bought Cathy some years ago.

"Well. And who do we have here?" Bill asked taking the girl's hand. "Certainly, another princess is attending the celebration?" Bill winked slyly at Jack. "You did not tell me that such an extraordinary young lady was your companion."

Alisha giggled. "Mrs. Pender sent me in here to tell you both that the party is about to begin."

"Hm," Bill said scratching his chin. "I guess we should all make our way into the dining room."

Bill and Fred stood up.

"Would you accompany us, Alisha?" Bill asked, bowing.

"I shall, " the girl said, standing up and grabbing her grandfather's and Bill's arms. The trio walked through the kitchen and into the dining room.

CHAPTER 7
Balloons, Buffoons and Ballasts

An explosion of water erupted from the Atlantic Ocean next to the Archaean Horizon, followed by another and then another. Bright yellow flotation devices were used to raise more relics from the salty grave the research ship hovered over. Some of the items were retrievable by the ship's submersible robotic, Aquabot. Some were too large, such as the ship's bell, its propellor, and the captain's strong box.

No treasure was expected from the old strong box. However, personal letters, logs, and other such items could be worth more than gold for a sea archaeologist if they remained intact. Deep within the bowels of the Archaean Horizon, in her laboratory, Dr. Roland Brambilla and his colleague Dr. Jeff Tarpon were pouring over the first recovery from their shipwreck discovery. The decades-old anchor had been cleaned enough to read the etchings on its rusting iron. True to its age, the hulk matched what the two had hypothesized upon finding the ship. The name on the anchor was a match: Constance.

"Roli. We found her." Jeff said, lifting his magnifying glass from the relic and looking at his friend.

"One of the many," Roli said.

"I've been after Constance for a very long time." Tarpon sighed. "And Roli…"

"Yes?"

"I have never spoken to you of this, but I have a personal attachment to this project," Jeff said tentatively.

"How so?"

"My only living Cousin Catherine, and she lives in Maine." Dr. Tarpon walked over and filled his coffee cup. "I do not think she knows I exist, mind you, but I have kept up with her career. Quite an exceptional young lady."

"Why are you telling me of this now?" Roli asked. "Are you going to tell her who you are?"

"No. I don't see the point. She has recently married." Jeff said, sitting. "A fiction writer if you will, a remarkably successful one. Bill Pender."

"I've heard of the man. And?"

"He married Catherine and has purchased the Shaw Estate."

"Captain Shaw from our wreck?" Roli asked surprised at this information.

"The same," Jeff said standing up and walking back to the anchor. "I wonder if that estate might have information about our wreck."

"How can an old house possibly have any connection to this wreck?"

"Maybe it is nothing. However, Catherine is a prominent historian for the southern part of Maine. She knows this area and its ghosts, Roli. And she lives in our captain's house. Captain Wilbur H. Shaw, the skipper of our wreck. And there is a library in that house within the widow's watch."

"And you think...?"

"I don't know what to think. I do know that the manor is intact, and there may be clues that can help us figure out why Constance went down with all hands. It is what we are doing here, is it not?"

"It is, Jeffery. That it is. And you never cease to amaze me. When do we leave?"

A loud pop was followed by another, and the Shaw Manor dining room was filled with children's laughter. The birthday party for Gaea Pender was in full swing, and both Bill and Cathy could not have been happier. Gaea had opened her presents, and the two dozen children that had come to celebrate with their friend had not gone unrewarded. Unbeknownst to Cathy, Bill had not forgotten his daughter's birthday and had outdone his wife by buying his daughter a puppy. The brindle boxer was charging about the dining room, ensuring she met every guest she came upon. The pup was a splendid surprise, but he had also purchased random gifts for all the children. "What," he had thought, "can make this party better?" Give gifts to all. Bill's idea had turned the party into a gala event. Cathy had frowned at first at being left out of her husband's quirky idea, but as the party unfolded, she could not help but smile and laugh.

"You are a scoundrel," Cathy whispered in her husband's ear.

Bill shrugged and responded softly, "I was getting tired of forgetting my beautiful daughter's birthday. And you know when I atone for something, I do it big."

"That you do, my love," Cathy said, fiddling with the large diamond ring on her finger.

"What are you going to name her?" A boy yelled over the din.

"Yes!" Vicky exclaimed. "She needs a name!"

"Butch!" One of the boys shouted.

"That's a boy's name." A girl said, laughing.

The group of kids and adults laughed as names were randomly called out. All except Gaea, who sat holding the puppy deep in thought. She stroked the soft fur of her new canine friend, who was barely eight weeks old. The puppy's eyes had still not fully changed to deep brown, and hints of newborn blue remained. Gaea ran her fingers over the green collar, and the dog chewed lightly on her finger.

"I know," Gaea said, looking up at her friends.

"Know what?" Vicky asked.

"I am going to wait until she tells me her name."

"Why?" Vicky asked.

"Because."

"Time and time again, I have to tell someone to do something, and how I want it done?" Bob Pepper asked himself gruffly. He slammed the door behind him, blew past his receptionist, and entered his office area. Storming through another door, he glared at his private secretary and charged into his office, flopping down behind his desk. He reached for a cigar, thought twice, and shut the box. Behind him, his secretary scurried after her boss and sat down facing him, minus the pen and notepad she normally would have had in her hands. "Sir?"

"Buffoons. All of them." Pepper said.

"Mr. Pepper?" Dorothy Smart asked again.

Pepper looked at his long-time personal secretary and laughed. "Dottie, only you can know when this old man needs more than…well, I can't hide anything from you, can I?"

"What do you mean?"

Pepper stood up and looked through the large windows offering a Manhattan view. "It's the damn doctors."

His secretary remained silent.

"The doctors," Pepper said. "Those idiots say I have pre-diabetes. I don't even eat sugary things!"

Dorothy took a deep breath and folded her hands in her lap. "Thank God."

Pepper sat down hard in his chair and slammed his fist onto his desk. "What?!"

"Bob." She began. "I was afraid it was cancer."

"What is the difference?" He asked as he stood again and began to pace the office. "I'm dead either way."

"No, you are not. Now you listen to me, Robert Franklin Pepper. Both of my parents died because of cancer in their lungs. They smoked themselves into a grave. That is why I hate those things." She said, pointing to the box of cigars on his desk. "I have diabetes. And I hate it. And so do millions of other people. You are nothing special, Robert. And you will live on, just like I do, and dozens like us right here in this company."

"You have this dreaded disease, Dottie? I had no idea."

"Me and many more."

"Who?"

Pepper's cell phone rang. He grabbed it, waving his secretary out of the office. "Pepper here, what is it?"

Dorothy closed the door quietly and paused, placing her ear up to it. "Thank you, and that is great news." She could hear Pepper say. "Yes, I'm grateful for keeping this under wraps. What's that? Oh yes, I will let people know when the time comes. Thank you again." She returned to her desk and tried to deal with her work. Something was not quite right in her office.

The weather had eased, but chilly rain continued to warm the Archaean Horizon's decks with water. Artifacts were being brought on board the research vessel at such a rate that the crew was struggling to handle them all. As on all archeologic finds and sites, whether land or underwater, all relics must be cataloged and managed with the utmost care, not damaging or destroying any evidence they might provide. Professor Mary Van Buren of the University of Nova Scotia had her hands full sorting through the artifacts as they were retrieved from the depths of the Atlantic. The simple expedition she had agreed upon had so far proven to be not so simplistic. An easy two-month sabbatical that would help her in authoring her latest book had taken a sudden turn into what she considered an equal to her first assignment as an intern on the Atocha discovery in the Florida Keys. That was in paradise. This find was in frigid waters; not only the Atlantic, but the weather had not cooperated.

"I need those pieces of wood tagged properly and taken down to lab three for soak preservation." Dr. Van Buren yelled over the wind.

"How's it going?" Roli Brambilla asked.

Van Buren looked up at the two men standing over her and frowned. "If it isn't Dr. Jekyll and Dr. Hyde." She said, standing to face the men. "What can I do for you two?"

"We have a lead that might help us with this discovery." Dr. Tarpon said.

"And?" Mary asked suspiciously.

"We have the name of the boat confirmed. She was the Constance, a fishing vessel under the command of Captain Wilbur H. Shaw. His manor is over on Cape Neddick in Maine, and we believe his personal library is intact."

"Marine archeologist to a librarian?" Mary Van Buren said with a laugh removing her rain-soaked gloves. "Where do I come in?"

"Both Roli and I are concerned with leaving the artifacts, shall I say, in the hands of babes. Supervision is needed." Jeff explained.

"So, you want me to stay behind and babysit?" Dr. Van Buren asked.

"On the contrary." Dr. Brambilla said. "That chore will fall to me. We need your expertise in this matter. Dr. Tarpon will be aiding you with investigating the library and the estate grounds. You have your PhD in Historical Archeology specializing in ancient and modern documents."

"Shit. I knew it. Librarian duty." Mary muttered.

CHAPTER 8
The Game

"Bill?" Cathy said, releasing her husband from a long embrace.

"Yeah, babe?" Bill answered, looking at his wife.

"I received an odd phone call at the shop. It was from a Dr. Tarpon, a Marine Archeologist. He claims he has found the wreck of the Constance."

"Captain Shaw's boat?" Bill asked.

"That is what he says. He thinks that we might be able to help him with his research into the wreck. He asked if he could stop by with a colleague and examine the library."

Bill released Cathy and stepped back, crossing his arms. "And?"

"Well, I told him he could. He is a scientist, after all, and you know my passion for these things."

Bill sighed and leaned against the kitchen counter, looking out at the Atlantic. "You know I don't like strangers showing up unannounced."

"It's not unannounced, Bill. He called and requested. And did so quite nicely." Cathy reassured him.

"Do I have to be here for this? Maybe I can take Gaea up to Fun Town for the day."

"No way. You must be here while they are in the library. And I don't think they know about the family cemetery, and you should be the one to take them there."

He turned and faced Cathy. "How much do we tell them? You know, about Tracy and the haunting?"

"Nothing. Dang Bill, these people are marine archeologists, not parapsychologists."

He laughed and pulled his wife back into his chest, kissing her. "You know I can never say no to you for any reason."

"C'mon, let's go. Our daughter is in the middle of a birthday party."

"Who?" Bill said, scratching his head and grinning.

"Get your ass in there." She said with a laugh.

The party lasted for the better part of the day ebbing only as the waxing moon began to reflect on the Atlantic waters. The friends of Gaea that remained numbered a handful of four. All those girls and their parents had permitted an impromptu sleepover. The girls had retired to Gaea's bedroom while the remaining adults sat in the great room sipping wine and cocktails, talking about the party and the birthday girl's possible choice of her new pet's name. Eventually, the subject of the suicide arose, and Bill and Cathy reluctantly had to deal with it.

Tracy Duchamp's suicide had made local news. However, phone calls by Pepper & Pepper and Bill's agent Clarissa had calmed the situation. There was the normal buzz, but it had dissipated quickly, and greased palms kept the story out of the national limelight. Even with the hush-hush, locals never seem to forget a happenstance that occurred in their community. Questions began to arise as the remaining adults sat and talked quietly next to the dying embers within the fireplace.

"Bill, what do you think she will name the dog?" Clarissa asked, taking a sip of her wine.

Bill shrugged and reached for his bottle of beer. "I can't say. She has her mother's intuition."

"And your creativity," Cathy remarked.

"It's a fine animal." Fred Black added, taking a drink of his water. "Boxers are extraordinary canines."

"Fred is right." Jackie Tamplan said, shifting herself on the arm of the sofa. "Incredible when it comes to protecting the family. Excellent choice, Bill."

"You could have consulted with me!" Cathy scolded her husband.

Bill smiled and stood up, walking to the fireplace. Reaching down, he picked up and tossed another log onto the embers.

"Cathy, I am so sorry about Tracy," Clarissa said somberly. "She seemed like such a sweet girl even though I only met her that one time at the housewarming."

Cathy sighed and picked up her wine glass. "She was my best friend. We grew up together. I believe it was an accident. She would never take her own life."

"Then why…"

The piano began to play, interrupting Jackie and startling the group. The sound was loud and not melodic. It was as if the keys were being punched down randomly. Cathy shrieked, and Bill headed toward the noise. The grand piano was situated in the room in such a way so as it could be played whilst guests sat listening and relaxing in the sitting area in front of the fireplace. The pianist would be facing the benefactors of music; thus, the keyboard was not visible to onlookers.

This was not the first time that Bill had heard a piano in the Shaw Manor start playing by itself. Memories struck deep within him as thoughts of what had happened over a decade ago permeated his mind. It was still difficult for Bill to grasp the fact that his house had been haunted by a truly angry ship captain and how the power of the captain's love had preserved the manor as he waited for his wife, Lily. Her passing had not extinguished that enthusiastic flame. Bill's best guess was that the couple had not been reunited through death. Captain Shaw had lost his life at sea; his wife could never accept her husband not ever coming home. He surmised that the souls were separated and unable to reunite, creating a paradox that confounded and, at times, terrified Bill Pender and his wife.

"What is it, Bill?!" David Woodley exclaimed, hopping the coffee table in pursuit of his host.

As Bill reached the piano, he tripped on a potted plant. The racket caused a startled Chimer to leap off the instrument's keys. Shrieking, the feline charged into the kitchen and vanished into the pantry. "Damn cat!" Bill said, rubbing his sore shin. David smiled sympathetically and followed Bill to the couch. Cathy held her hand over her mouth as she giggled. The rest of the guests laughed as well, all except for Bill, who was clearly angry. "I have told Gaea a hundred times to close that piano when she is not playing it," Bill said, sitting on the sofa.

Cathy snuggled up to her husband and took over the chore of rubbing his shin. "Honey," She whispered into his ear. "She did close it."

He looked at his wife. "Bill, I watched her close the piano's fallboard," Cathy repeated. "And she locked it." The rain began to fall harder, splashing against the manor's windows. Thunder rolled in the distance.

An Agusta Bell AB 412 helicopter sat warming up on the deck of the Archaean Horizon. Once considered a fine choice for a corporate aircraft, this 1981 model had seen better days. Although it had been maintained to FAA standards and the electronics and engine were in acceptable shape, the interior had not seen such care. The helicopter normally could accommodate thirteen passengers plus one flight attendant. Six of the seats had been removed to allow for more scientific cargo. The remaining showed signs of wear as fading fabric gave way to rips and tears. The aircraft windows were starting to yellow, and Dr. Mary Van Buren did not like the moaning and groaning that the Agusta Bell was emitting.

"I hate to fly." She said, fastening her seatbelt. "Scientific research should call for a better plane. Are you sure this bucket of bolts is safe?"

"Mary," Dr. Tarpon said softly, tapping his colleague's arm, "I have flown in this dozens of times and can assure you that we will get to our destination safely. The flight to the Sanford Airport is short. We will be there before you know it."

Mary's fear of flight was not unfounded. She had traveled extensively, as her father was a Pan-Am captain who flew flights worldwide. As an eight-year-old traveling with her parents and her twin brother, most destinations were available to the family if her father went to the airport and filed the proper paperwork to include them. It was all free airfare as a benefit to airline employees.

During a family flight to Cairo, the fear of flying was ingrained into a sixteen-year-old Mary. The flight had originated from Boston, and the weather had not been favorable for the last leg of the trip. Turbulence had started to toss the Boeing 747 shortly before the descent into Cairo International Airport. The aircraft had come close to a belly land due to the landing gear's near failure to deploy. The incident had terrified Mary and after being forced to board the return flight, the girl had sworn off flying. Until her career choice demanded it, once she graduated and became an archeologist, the thought of having to travel to the next project site terrified her. Her love for her profession, however, drove her past her fear.

"I certainly hope so," Mary said, closing her eyes and gripping Tarpon's arm as the helicopter's engines revved and it lifted from the ship. Turning, it sped toward the rocky coastline of Maine.

Gaea's new puppy had played herself out and was curled up near the girl's feet. As the dog snored loudly, its eyelids fluttered, lost in dreams.

"She is so adorable," Alisha said, touching the dog lightly behind her ears.

"I've been begging my dad for a puppy for so long," Julia said. "He thinks I'm too young."

"I think everyone should have a puppy," Victoria said. My dad asked me if I wanted one, but my mom had just died, so I told him no."

"Why?" Gaea asked. "Puppies make everyone happy!"

"What if it died? It would be my fault." Victoria answered.

Gaea frowned and took her friend's hand. "I told you, Victoria, it is not your fault that your mom died."

Victoria stood up and clenched her fists. "I told you, Gaea, my name is Vicky. Not Victoria!"

"But I thought that was only for me."

Victoria sat down, crossing her legs. "I changed my mind. From now on, I want all my friends to call me Vicky."

The girls rolled their eyes and laughed.

"Everyone okay with that?" Gaea asked, giggling.

"I like Victoria, but it is her name," Julia said.

"Yes," Alisha said, nodding her head.

"It's settled then," Gaea announced. "Victoria shall now be called Vicky."

"What shall we play then?" Alisha asked, trying to change the subject.

"I know." Julia offered. "Let's play Truth or Dare. That's a fun game."

"How do you play it?" Gaea asked.

"It's easy. We take turns. I will ask, hmm, maybe, Alisha: Truth or Dare? She then will choose one of the two. If she says the truth, then she has to answer my question with no lies. She must be honest.

If she chooses to dare, then I would get to tell her to do something that she might not want to do. But she can't refuse. That is the game." Julia explained.

"I want to go first!" Vicky demanded.

"We choose; you know, to see who goes first. Gaea, we need to print our names on a piece of paper. Can we do that?"

"I have paper and drawing pencils. Will that work, Julia?"

"Yes. Now we need something to put the names in. A hat, a bag, something like that."

"How about this?" Alisha asked, taking the pillow she was sitting on and removing the cover.

"Perfect. Gaea, can you write them?"

"Here, everyone, take a pencil and piece of paper and write your own name." She replied.

"I want a blue one," Vicky said, pulling a pencil from the box.

"I'll take green!" Alisha exclaimed.

The girls quickly scribbled their names on a piece of paper. Crumpling them up, they tossed them into the pillowcase. Alisha twisted the fabric and shook it above her head.

"OK, who gets to pick the first one?" Julia asked.

"Gaea, of course," Vicky said. "It's her party, after all."

Alisha opened the pillowcase and held it out for Gaea. She reached into it and pulled a crumpled piece of paper from its depths. The girls gasped as she unfolded it and held it up for all to see.

"Vicky!" They all shrieked.

The guests bid Bill goodbye and left, climbing into their respective vehicles. The rain had picked up and become a downpour. Melting snow caused streams of icy, muddy water to rush down the driveway. He closed the front door and walked to the kitchen, where Cathy and Clarissa were finishing the remainder of the glasses. Doug sat stoically, gazing into the fire.

"You have been quiet tonight," Bill said, taking a seat.

"Just taking it all in." His friend said with a deep sigh. "Clarissa wants kids. Did you know that, Bill?" Thunder cracked loudly followed by a bright flash of lightning that lit up the sheen of torrential rain striking the mansion's windows.

"You are second guessing?"

"Having children is a ton of responsibility. I'm not sure I'm ready for that challenge. Were you?" Doug asked, looking at Bill.

"You're kidding. I was terrified when Cathy told me she was pregnant." Bill said, glancing over at his wife. "I think the excitement overtook the fear after I had a chance to let it all sink into my brain. Once it sank in, the reality of becoming a father became exciting. And time consuming."

"How so?"

"Cathy decided on natural childbirth, so no drugs. But there are classes to take as a couple, especially if you want to be in the delivery room."

"You did that?"

"You bet," Bill said, smiling. "I would never miss the opportunity to witness my daughter being born. How about one more beer?"

"Sure," Doug said, handing his empty bottle to him. Standing up, Bill heard a loud, high-pitched scream come from upstairs.

"That was not laughter," Doug said, standing up as well.

CHAPTER 9
A Dare & A Dodgy Approach

Thunder crashed outside, causing the girls to gasp—all except Vicky. Determined, the girl called out, "Julia, truth or dare."

"Why me?"

"Because I get to choose."

"Fine. I'm not afraid to play. Truth!"

Vicky rolled her eyes and thought. "Let me see. I see how you look at Danny at school. Julia, have you kissed him?"

"Gross! You have to be kidding. That creep. Really?"

"So did you?"

"No! That is so disgusting. Have you seen how he eats his Sloppy Joes?" Julia asked while scrunching up her face.

The girls laughed, and their game nearly turned into a pillow fight. The Boxer awoke, stood, stretched, and peed on the floor promptly.

"Gaea, your dog!" Alisha exclaimed. "Now that is gross."

Gaea reached for a bath towel lying on her bed and wiped up the small puddle left by the dog. "She's a puppy. Give her a break."

"It's still disgusting," Alisha said.

"She is adorable. And Gaea is right. A puppy will piddle." Julia added.

"Wait!" Gaea exclaimed. "That is her name! Piddles!"

"You are going to name your dog because she peed on the floor? Really?"

"Of course." Gaea started to explain. "My dad told me that when he is writing, the characters he writes about sometimes come from things that can happen in real life. Things just like this can be the best name! Julia, you are a genius!"

"So, Piddles the Boxer dog?" Julia asked.

"I love it," Vicky said.

"Me too!" Alisha exclaimed.

"Ok, now that's settled, Julia, I think it is your turn to draw a name," Gaea concluded.

"I still want a puppy," Julia said, reaching into the bag. She drew another crumpled piece of paper, unfolded it, and held it up. Vicky.

The Bell helicopter caught a brief thunderstorm during its flight to Sanford Airport, turbulence adding to the collective bounce on its final descent to the tarmac. Dr. Van Buren gripped her colleague's knee and gasped, squeezing hard. "What the hell was that?"

"Just a little turbulence, Mary. We are nearly on the ground."

"This is the last time I am flying in this bucket of bolts!"

Jeff Tarpon smiled reassuringly. "It's our only way back to the Archaean Horizon."

"I'll swim."

The helicopter circled and hovered momentarily before gently touching down on the ground. Tarpon looked out the scratched window. They had landed near what appeared to be a World War II-style hanger, although it seemed to be well maintained. Small, fixed-wing aircraft were neatly parked inside. He could see people doing various tasks in and around the hangar. Three men were attending to his helicopter, motioning with sticks that had no meaning to the doctor.

The captain appeared and smiled at his passengers. "Here we are, safe and sound. Sorry about the bumpy approach. You can debark in a moment. Best to let the rotors wind down. Mighty windy if you don't." The duo shouldered their packs and briefcases and exited out onto the tarmac. "Our ride should be here soon." Dr. Tarpon said. "I'm surprised it's not already here."

"This is southern Maine?" She spoke. "It looks like Kansas. Flat and dry."

"Sanford is a small town, and this part of it suffered a devastating brush fire years ago. It is still recovering. As we move toward the coast you will see the beauty, especially when we reach the coast. And if we had the time, back to the west is a town called Springvale. A quaint little village that still has the ghosts of textile mills and a history that one can become lost in."

"Perhaps. But it's certainly not northern Maine. And where is our limo?"

"On our budget?" Dr. Tarpon laughed, pointing toward a taxi driving down the road toward the two. "Welcome to the glamorous world of research."

"I hope we at least get to eat on our shoestring budget. I am sick of ship food, and if you take me to a pizza parlor, I will kill you."

"That, my dear, is covered. I have reservations about a lovely place right on Wells Beach. You may sup on the wonderful seafood from the frigid waters of Maine."

The cab pulled up, and a young woman jumped out. "Luggage?" she asked.

"No," Tarpon answered. "Just a day trip."

"Great!" the driver replied, opening the rear door of the Buick. The researchers climbed into the car, followed by their driver.

"So, where to?" She asked.

"The Longshoreman in Ogunquit," Tarpon said.

"I love that place!" Their driver exclaimed. "By the way, my name is Laurie."

"Nice to meet you, Laurie," Mary said. "I just hope you drive better than our pilot can fly." Tarpon rolled his eyes and looked out the window as the taxi drove down the road leading to route one hundred and nine and the coast.

"Vicky!" The girls yelled.

"How is that possible?" She said, feeling uncomfortable with being the focus of attention again. "Why does my name get called?"

"It's random," Alisha said, laughing. "Do you think every piece of paper in the bag has your name on it?"

"No. It's just weird."

"So, darling, truth or dare?"

"She's afraid," Julia said.

"I am not! Dare, so there."

"Oh." The girls said together.

"Well, let's see. I dare you to go up to the tower and stay there for five minutes."

"Wait," Gaea said, interrupting. "She can't go there."

"Why not?" Alisha asked.

"Dreamer's hideaway is off limits. It's my dad's private place."

"My dad told me it was a widow's watch," Julia said. "And someone died up there."

"What is a widow's watch?" Alisha asked.

"I'm not sure," Gaea answered. "But the tower is my father's private office, so we can't go up there. He writes his stories in his library. Even I am not allowed to go to his dreamer's hideaway. And I have never heard of anyone dying up there."

"I get it," Victoria added. "My dad won't let me near the garage. He says it's dangerous."

"So, Julia, you have to choose another dare," Gaea said.

"Well, let me see." She thought for a moment. "I know! Vicky, I dare you to go up to the attic and stay there for five minutes!"

Vicky's eyes grew wide then she squinted. "You think I am afraid, don't you? Well, I'm not. Where is it? You scaredy cats can stay here; I will go explore the attic."

Vicky stood up and walked into the hallway.

"Two doors down on the left!" Gaea called after her friend.

Vicky closed the bedroom door and walked slowly until she stood in front of a large door.

Cathy and Bill had restored the manor lovingly and were able to save parts of the home. The chestnut doors were something that Cathy had focused on. All the portals in the manor were crafted of solid wood, ornate, and extremely heavy. They were also taller in comparison. A full foot taller than a typical modern door. Four large hinges were required to support their weight, yet they opened and closed easily with a gentle push. The iron hinges and the brass knobs and lock sets had been meticulously restored by some of Maine's best locksmiths and craftsmen. Cathy had called upon her contacts in her field of antiquities and archeology to have every aspect of the doors restored to their former glory.

Vicky looked up and down the empty hallway. She could hear the adults' laughing downstairs. She grasped the doorknob, and as she turned it, lightning lit the window at the end of the hall. A clap of thunder followed that seemed to shake the house. She heard her friends shriek at the noise as she opened the door. The stairs to the attic were narrow and climbed steeply upward, fading into partial darkness. Vicky felt along the wall, finding a switch. She turned it on, and a pale-yellow light flickered on at the top of the stairs. She sighed and climbed up onto the first step. "You can do this, Vicky." She said to herself. "We are up in our attic all the time. It's just another space to explore. Nothing to be afraid of."

"Now, this is more like it," Mary said.

The taxi had turned down the stretch of road that cut through a salt marsh flanking the north side of Wells Beach. She could smell the air, which, although partially made up of rotting seaweed, still created a pleasant scent as it mixed with the spray of the Atlantic Ocean. The weather had started to warm up, releasing the promise of spring.

The road curved down from route one and afforded a spectacular view of the rocky shoreline of Maine to the south with a vast stretch of beach to the north. Directly ahead, Mary could see what seemed to be a small area of buildings, one large one that appeared to be a hotel. The parking lot stood nearly empty as most of the businesses had shut for the winter. Essential businesses stayed open to cater to the locals. The Longshoreman was one such establishment that opened early as it prepared for the droves of people that came during the summer months.

"I came here often as a child." Dr. Tarpon said. "My parents adored Maine. And I did as well. I was born in Montreal. Did you know that?"

"No, you never mentioned it."

"Maine was an inexpensive getaway being so close. Five hours and we were here. The hotels were cheap back then. I remember my father saying that. And the food was incredible. Lobster, full-bellied fried clams, haddock, steamed mussels. I could go on and on. I made so many friends here in Maine."

The taxi pulled into the parking lot and parked near the entrance of the restaurant.

"So, you chose this restaurant out of nostalgia?" Mary asked.

"Partially. There is not much open yet this time of year. Tourist season hasn't quite started yet."

"I see."

Laurie opened the door and let her passengers out. Jeff pulled his wallet out and started fishing for money. "How much?"

"I tell you what. I know you must go somewhere after this so why don't I wait for you? I'm hungry, and I'll grab a bite. It's slow, and I have no other calls. And don't worry, I'll turn the meter off." Laurie informed them.

"What do you think?" Mary asked her companion. "It's your dime."

"Good for me. An hour then?"

"Perfect!" Laurie said. "See you then!"

Tarpon watched the young driver skip off toward the restaurant, her dark hair dancing in the brisk wind. "Who has eyes that blue?" Jeff asked himself.

"We better get inside. I think another round of thunderstorms are on the way."

"Lead the way," Mary said, grasping Jeff's arm.

CHAPTER 10
Montreal & The Archaean Horizon

Ten-year-old Jeffery Tarpon charged into his house and ran toward his mother, who was finishing the morning dishes. She turned and looked at her son as he sat down at the kitchen table. "Slow down before you hurt yourself." she scolded.

Emily Tarpon was a typical housewife in the late 1950s. She was a stay-at-home mom. However, her natural beauty had nearly led her to a career in acting. She had spent her youth acting in high school plays and productions and singing in the school and church choirs. Emily was a gifted student, maintaining a straight A average throughout academics. Her Irish father had been a strict disciplinarian and a church pastor. Her upbringing had created a false shell that Emily lived in. Even though she was considered one of the most popular girls in school, she had few friends. She had inherited her father's fiery red hair and piercing blue eyes. Nearly every boy in school dreamt of being her consort. Few even tried. Those that did face the wrath of her father. It wasn't until her father's death that she began to experience the world as a teenager.

As a junior in high school, Emily became infatuated with a young man named Jonathan, who was always engrossed in his writing. Most girls ignored the boy. He had dark hair, wore glasses, and his nose was crooked. Emily found him fascinating. She tried numerous times to engage the lad in conversation, yet he seemed shy and aloof. His head was always buried in a notebook with a pen in hand. When she tried to look at his writing, he would slam the book closed and scurry off with a weak apology. Emily was not a girl to be deterred, and after learning that Jonathan was a member of the writing club, she promptly joined. She had little luck with the young man until the start of her senior year. She and Jonathan were chosen to lead the effort to create the school's yearbook.

As time passed, Jonathan seemed to warm up to Emily and finally worked up the courage to ask her to go with him to a book signing by a local writer. She jumped at his invitation and had the time of her life listening to the author's speech and then holding Jonathan's hand as they stood in line for him to sign his book. She beamed with happiness seeing him smile and laugh excitedly, showing the author's signature to her. "Look! He wrote my name!" He had exclaimed.

"Wow, Jonathan!" She replied, wrapping her arms around his neck. Stunned, the boy looked at her and smiled. She smiled back and kissed him.

Jeffery Tarpon was born to Mr. and Mrs. Jonathan Tarpon eight years later. His father's passion for knowledge was evident in the young man and his mother's natural gift of the arts. Science and creativity merged when Jeffery decided to pursue a career in marine archeology, and his parents could not have been prouder of their son. Jeffery had never been a shy boy and was active in several activities in school. Running for school president and winning the seat had been the apex of his achievements. Being multi-lingual had been a boon. Growing up in Montreal, Canada, speaking French was a given; however, with his mother's influence, he quickly grasped English and Latin. He was a natural leader and well-liked by his fellow students.

Numerous girlfriends had not come to anything but long and caring friendships. Entering the University of Alberta for his undergraduate studies, he became attracted to other boys. It was during his four-year stay that he came to grips with his sexuality. His studies kept him from acting upon his desires as he concentrated on them with a relentless passion.

Upon graduation with a PhD from the University of Massachusetts, Jeffery once again put his personal life aside and dove headlong into a project funded by the Jacques-Yves Cousteau Maritime Research Project. He found it fascinating to merge traditional archeology with the sea's mysteries. He volunteered at once and was grateful for the small salary that was offered. The experience, he reasoned, would be worth more than a dozen degrees. Especially when collaborating with the esteemed oceanographer Cousteau.

Les Pièges de la Mer was to be the project that set Jeffery on his quest to become what he became, a world-renowned maritime archeologist. Exploring the Grand Banks of his native country of Canada in Nova Scotia had set the course for the young scientist. Not long after completing the project and being a part of the discoveries, Dr. Tarpon was offered the position of Professor of Maritime Archelogy at the prestigious University of Massachusetts. A few years later, he was on a sabbatical, applying for grants and organizing his own expeditions into the depths of the world's vast waters, hunting for the ghosts of long-lost shipwrecks.

His efforts had not gone unnoticed by his peers within the scientific community. Dr. Tarpon's research and discoveries have been published by esteemed organizations like the Archaeological Institute of America. He was awarded as an elected member of the American Philosophical Society and held The George Fletcher Bass Merit of Honor from the University of New York. Tarpon's accomplishments mounted quickly and if it were not for the death of his mother, his career may not have arrived at the apex that he had strived for.

As an only child, inheriting his family estate proved to be the final key to his success. The pain of losing his mother was the equivalent of "Having his heart torn out and thrown into a pigsty, " he once told Roli. Emptying the old home and selling off the family belongings was beyond difficult. True to the man's fortitude, Tarpon looked to the future again.

He sold the estate for a tidy sum and bought the Norrsken, an aging Swedish icebreaker that would become his home for the next two decades. The ship needed a full refit; however, Tarpon chose the old ship for its thick hull. After years of service in the Arctic, the Norrsken was retired by the Svenska marinen. The old ship measured at nearly 120 meters and displaced over 15,000 tons. She had ample room on her aft for the helo deck to be retrofitted for the helicopter the scientist planned on purchasing. Again, although another older piece of equipment, Bell helicopters were proven to be extremely dependable even in foul weather. Tarpon purchased the Swedish icebreaker and sent it to dry dock for a refit. He had chosen NORYARDS BMV in Norway to do the job. One of many that occurred over the following years.

Once the refit was complete, the Norrsken was re-christened the Archaean Horizon. Tarpon had chosen to hire an older Swedish cruise ship captain. Lars Enstrom had grown tired of taking passengers from one port of call to another. The voyages had become a dull routine that repeated itself to the point of madness. He wanted something more adventurous. When Dr. Jeffery Tarpon proposed the captainship of the Archaean Horizon to the seasoned skipper he had jumped at the chance. The salary was nearly the same as his former cruise line was paying and he didn't really need the money. He had saved and invested enough to retire comfortably when he was ready. And Capt. Lars Enstrom was not ready to hang up his hat. His first duty was the first voyage of the research vessel. An expedition into the North Sea for sunken World War II German warships. Although a fair trial voyage, the expedition's results were less than desirable for the captain and his young boss. It wasn't until Roli joined the crew that the Archaean Horizon's luck improved.

Dr. Roli Brambilla became Tarpon's colleague, and as some suspected, maybe more. All rumors aside, the pair were undeniably professional when together, and none questioned their choice to share a cabin when at sea. The addition of Roli also brought well-needed funds. His family's vast wealth contributed to the oceanographic research the two had a passion for, making their endeavors easier and more enjoyable. Dr. Jeffery Tarpon could not have chosen a better partner.

The Archaean Horizon's new "family" had evolved over the years. She was filled with colleagues, students undergoing internships, technicians, and a crew that kept the research vessel doing what it was designed and christened for: discovery.

Dr. Tarpon also received help from companies and universities. CAT Diesel had provided new experimental bio-diesel engines for the Archaean Horizon, along with a technical crew to keep them working and to study their performance, allowing the ship's chief engineer to spend more time with other functions of the ship. Students from MIT, with permission from the esteemed university, gave the Aquabot submersible to Tarpon's deep sea exploration missions with the agreement that members of an MIT scientific team would see to its functionality and maintenance and that the school would have first rights to study the data the submersible collected. After this, Dr. Tarpon's team would have ample time for analysis as the mission primary researchers. Jeffery had immediately agreed to all the offers. He had limited expertise regarding some of the advanced scientific equipment loaded on his vessel.

Now, years after the Archaean Horizon's christening, the research team was on an important mission funded by the Oceanographic Society of Canada and the Maine State Maritime Association. This included a large grant from the Smithsonian Institution. The anchor that presently sat in an acid bath in a laboratory on the ship was highly desirable for the Smithsonian's new maritime wing. All was well on the Archaean Horizon.

Mary and Jeff sat sipping an after-lunch aperitif, gazing at the Atlantic Ocean. Dark clouds were rolling in from the east, and they could see flashes of light within them.

"My grandmother used to call that heat lightning," Mary commented, setting her glass on the table.

"I believe mine did as well." He answered. "It was an omen of a storm to come. They just didn't realize that it was a violent storm on the horizon."

"Sometimes, the storm stayed in the distance and simply drifted until it went out of sight." He paused, then added, "Or it dissipated."

"You think the ship is OK?"

Tarpon laughed and took a sip of his drink. "With Lars at the helm? If he had been the captain of the Lusitania, it would not have sunk. He is a man who knows his craft."

"I would agree. Quite brilliant. Why is he not married?" Mary asked.

"A man like him is married to the oceans," Jeffery said. "Lars told me he wishes to be buried at sea. I agreed if he is still the captain of the Archaean Horizon."

"How old is he?"

"I believe Lars recently turned 77."

"I would never guess a day over fifty," Mary said, surprised.

"He is not unlike the man we are going to research. Captain Wilbur H. Shaw. Or so I'm hypothesizing."

"The Constance captain." Mary acknowledged with a nod of her head.

"Yes. It takes a certain kind of man to give his soul to the sea."

"Ah, but Captain Shaw was married."

"That he was, but his true love was the sea, and it was there that he met his demise," Jeff stated somberly.

"Quite sad." She agreed.

"Perhaps. We don't know much about the good captain. I'm hoping we will learn more at the Shaw Manor."

"I see. Sometimes a shipwreck's greatest secret is not its cargo, nor its broken hull, or treasures, but the souls that served upon it."

"Well said, Doctor Van Buren." Tarpon acknowledged holding his glass up to toast his colleague. "That is why you are here."

CHAPTER 11
A Celebration & The Beach

Robert Pepper sat in his office holding a proof of a novel that was written by one of his favorite employees. He ran his hand over the sleek gloss cover of the paperback. He fanned through the pages, closing his eyes, taking in the fresh ink and paper scent. Closing the book, he read the cover. The title was as striking as its contents. The author was a natural writer and a genius in his style of storytelling. Horror was not one of the editor's personal choice of genres. However, it sold, and this book kept him up the entire night, second-guessing his beliefs.

The Etchings Within the Vatican's Catacombs by Jack William Jefferson. A catchy and daunting title, he surmised. Pepper turned the book over in his hands, looking for imperfections. He could find none. The art department had done a marvelous job on the cover design and Bob was sure that the lad would be happy with the results. Who wouldn't be? The subject matter would be controversial, the editor reasoned. The Catholic Church would probably have an issue with a sitting pope being portrayed as a demon. It was fiction, and if it pissed off a few people, who gave a shit? Bob Pepper could smell a bestseller, and he was holding one in his hands.

The Editor-in-Chief of Pepper & Pepper was about to launch a campaign to promote the book and a promising career for the young man. Jack was about to get a retainer check and a contract. Bill Pender had another signing coming up soon, and if the editor had his way, young Jack would tag along. Looking up, he admired the large oil painting of his father that adorned the wall. Dr. Adam Edison Pepper had founded the company and had trained his son in all aspects of publishing. Upon his early death at 54 years old, fresh out of college, Robert took the reins of his father's dream. For the most part, he had been successful until ill fortune hit the company. The loss of writers to other publishers and periodical publications and magazines going under had nearly left the company in ruins. Numerous factors led to the problems. People were just not buying books that were printed on paper as much as they had. Newspapers were going out of business with the advent of the digital age. The internet dominated the stock market, and print publications suffered. He remembered when his father was furious with what television was doing to his industry. The news was conveyed live in black and white or living color, and tomorrow's newspaper was becoming passe.

The publishing company persevered with Bill Pender's signing and his becoming one of the most successful authors in the world. Pepper & Pepper saw a resurgence in sales, authors, and new magazines. New projects in internet publication development arrived and resulted in creating a new department. E-books might be the wave of the future. Through it all, the company was now rejecting potential writers instead of begging for them. Bob reached over and pressed his intercom button. "Are we ready to surprise Jack?"

"Yes, sir." His secretary answered. "I sent him to the other side of the plant on an errand. It will give us time to get prepared. In fact, we are ready. The only thing I'm waiting for is the catering company to come up from the lobby and set up in the conference room."

"You are the best. Let me know. And when you page him, make it sound like he is in trouble."

"You are an evil man," Dorothy said with a giggle. "Oh, you still need to sign his check."

Jack was not an individual to waste time. Yet, for the life of him, he could not fathom why he was being sent the length of two city blocks that made up the factory to retrieve a maintenance procurement document that could have easily been delivered by one of the company's in-house couriers. Not that he minded. Such a task led him through the heart of the building. He particularly enjoyed walking along the glass-enclosed catwalk that ran the length of "P Section." The walkway was built along the ceiling and afforded a bird's eye view of the various books and magazines as they rolled off dozens of printing presses that filled the floor. The massive rolls of paper that were constantly being moved and tied to the machines astonished the aspiring novelist. "One day." Jack would tell himself. "My book will be rolling off those presses."

He had been more than surprised when his boss, Mr. Pepper, agreed to read his manuscript. Jack knew it was good but had reservations that it would live up to the Pepper & Pepper standards of excellence. He reached the end of the building section and pressed the elevator button. Four stories below, a glass-enclosed lift began to climb to pick up its passenger. The door slid open, and Jack stepped inside. Only two sides of the cube were glass. The two stainless steel panels hid the mechanical workings that made an OTIS elevator work. Jack pressed the "G" button, and it glided silently toward the work floor below.

Dr. Mary Van Buren had insisted on taking a short walk along the beach after lunch. Steamed mussels and pan-seared sea scallops were perfect with the light Pino Greccio wine that Jeffery Tarpon had chosen. Even the lightly toasted artisan bread was perfect for sopping up the sauce that lingered underneath the empty shells. With time to kill before heading to the Shaw Estate, he had gladly agreed. As the two walked along the beach of Ogunquit, seagulls squawked above them as the building waves of the Atlantic crashed upon the shore.

"That storm is coming in," Tarpon said, taking Mary's arm.

She looked to the east. Ominous clouds swirled in the distance, and low rumbles of thunder filled her ears. Hints of blue were rapidly being covered by another bout of Mother Nature's wrath dressed in gray and black.

"We have to get back to Laurie soon. We are expected at the Shaw Manor."

"Let the girl have a break," Mary said. "I told her we would be ready to leave soon. The extra twenty I gave her seemed to make her happy."

"I thought you were a poor scientist."

"With what you are paying me?" She laughed. "I'm using part of my grant money."

"As it stands, we will only have a couple of hours for introductions. The actual research will start in the morning." Tarpon stooped and picked up a shell, long turned into an archeologic remnant from a time in the distant past.

"Collecting a souvenir?"

"It always fascinates me how the ocean can bring back to us a creature that once lived millions of years ago."

"A reminder, perhaps?" Mary said, looking up at Jeffery.

"Or a warning. We are all creatures. Our species will be on this planet for a fragment of time. As per the clock of the universe."

"I'm unsure if you are extremely astute, Dr. Jeffery Tarpon, or simply obtuse."

He turned and faced his colleague as heavy raindrops began to pelt them. "Mary, I would never consider another scientist to help me on this project. You are an outstanding and brilliant woman."

"Great, now let's get back. We are about to get poured on, " she said, grabbing his arm. The two ran back to the Longshoreman and achieved cover as the skies opened.

"Jack Jefferson," Dorothy said sharply over the Pepper & Pepper intercom. "Report at once to the conference room on the executive level. Jack Jefferson, report without delay!" The secretary turned the microphone off and set it on the desk. "Was that harsh enough?" She asked her boss.

"And you call me evil." Bob Pepper said, laughing. "That kid should be here in less than five minutes." Before biting, he picked up a raw carrot and dipped it into a creamy sauce. "Delicious."

Jack nearly tripped when the announcement came over the plant's speakers. He climbed back into the elevator and pushed the button that sent the elevator gliding back up toward the plant's ceiling.

"What have you done now, Jack?" He asked himself. That had been Dorothy, and she sounded cross. He felt that he was in trouble but had no idea why. He performed his duties diligently and never had so much formal complaint. The rantings of his boss came as a given. Being the personal gofer for such a man came with its issues. Robert Pepper was demanding but always fair and even mumbled a thank you from time to time. He could come to no logical reason for why he was to be reprimanded. Yet, Jack ran back as fast as he could to the woman who had sent him on an errand. An errand, he reminded himself, that he had not completed.

He reached the executive wing of the plant and slid around a corner, nearly falling and colliding with the conference doors. The heavy double oak doors were emblazoned with P&P on them. They had massive brass hinges, four per door, and accented ornate doorknobs, also exquisitely crafted from solid brass. Jack had spent hours polishing the metal as a young intern to keep it shining and up to the owner's standards. He pressed his ear to a door, but all he could hear was muted conversation. The thick doors were designed for privacy. He reached to knock on the door just as it swung open. Bob Pepper grabbed the young man's hand and pulled him into the room.

"Surprise!" A chorus of voices greeted him.

He stood stunned, looking around the large room. He recognized and knew all the people. The ensemble consisted of executives, editors, design specialists, and others that Jack knew as talent scouts. The heads of Pepper's sales department and the newly formed internet division were also present. Dorothy Smart stood smiling next to Pepper.

"I didn't get the paperwork you sent me for." Jack apologized.

"The older woman approached him and smiled again. "That was just a red herring, my dear."

"A red herring indeed!" Pepper said loudly. "And now for the reason we are gathered here!"

CHAPTER 12
Manor's Manner

The top of the stairs ended in a space illuminated by a pale-yellow incandescent light bulb. Vicky was terrified at the thought of what was at the top of the stairs.

She did not show her fear to her friends. The girl had always been afraid and hid her feelings well. Her father had become a drunk after her mother's death, and more than once, he had taken his anger out on his daughter. He had never touched her to cause her harm. However, the verbal abuse had caused Victoria to withdraw into shadows that the girl found both comforting and terrifying. Being yelled at was one thing, locked in the attic as punishment had been the worst. Left alone in the darkness for hours at a time was Vicky's worst nightmare. And this dare from Julia could not have been more horrific, unbeknownst to her friends. Yet, she was not one to back down.

The friendships that had grown over the months brought the young girl back into the light. She adored one of her new friends more than the others. Gaea had taught her what respect meant. Vicky had exposed her innermost thoughts and even told her friend that she hated her name, Victoria. Gaea openly embraced Victoria and loved her choice of Vicky. Now, she had friends that accepted her for who she was. Friends that understood, or at least seemed to understand, the pain that came with the abuse. Vicky knew that none of her friends had experienced what she did, and Gaea especially had no problems such as hers. Somehow, her friend had empathy and cared deeply for what happened in Victoria's life. Feelings that Vicky had never understood until she met Gaea.

Being part of Gaea's birthday party was the highlight of her life. But agreeing to play this cursed game was bringing up feelings of dread and fear that she so wanted to forget. A dare was a dare, even if it meant that she had to climb the stairs in an old manor and confront her deepest fears. Slowly, Vicky crept up the narrow stairwell.

"That was so not cool, Julia," Gaea said.

"Why not? A dare is a dare."

"Just because. Vicky is terrified of attics."

"How was I supposed to know? We are playing a stupid game, aren't we? And it's only five minutes. She will be back soon."

"That attic is creepy. My mom told me to keep out of it."

"So, have you?" Alisha asked.

"Have I what?" Gaea replied, annoyed.

"Stayed out of the attic?"

The birthday girl gripped a pillow tight to her chest. "There is something up there, and it seems bad. Really bad. I won't go near that place. It scares me."

"Then why is Vicky going up there?" Julia said. "Why didn't you tell us?"

Gaea shrugged as a sharp scream from Vicky came from above.

Bill and Doug ran for the grand staircase and charged up. Bill slipped and hit his head on the railing. Doug reached back and pulled the now cursing and bleeding Bill up the second flight of stairs. Behind the duo, Cathy and Clarissa followed closely. Once they reached the hallway, three young girls stood with very worried looks on their faces.

"What the hell?" Bill said, approaching his daughter.

Gaea pointed. "We were playing a game. Vicky went up to the attic."

Cathy knelt in front of her and held her shoulders. "I told you to stay out of there. It's not safe."

Bill threw open the attic door and charged up the stairs. A moment later he reappeared holding a shaking, crying, and scratched Vicky in his arms.

"It was the cat," Vicky said, sobbing.

Bill examined the girl's arm and looked at his wife. The wound was not dissimilar to what Cathy had experienced years before. She had sworn that the cat that had attacked her in the attic was not Chimer. A fact that Bill had a tough time to dispute since their cat was found sound asleep on the grand piano. And there was the issue with Chimer's eyes. A fact neither he nor his wife could rectify in their discussions.

"It's just a simple scratch. It's not even bleeding. Still, maybe I should call her father."

"No!" Gaea and Vicky said in unison.

"Please, Mr. Pender. I am fine. Don't send me home. I want to stay here with Gaea."

"Daddy, please!" Gaea pleaded. Julia and Alisha nodded in agreement. "It wasn't her fault, daddy. We were playing Truth or Dare."

Clarissa rolled her eyes and crossed her arms. "Been there and done that. I never liked playing it."

"Gaea," Cathy began hugging her daughter, "It's your first sleepover and you have to take care of your friends. Don't try dumb things. Me and dad tell you not to do certain things for reasons. We don't want to see you get hurt. Like staying away from the sea wall out back. OK?"

"I'm sorry, Mom. I love Vicky. It was my fault."

"OK, the show is over," Bill said, turning off the attic light and closing the door. "No more silly games. Besides, it is bedtime. Back to Gaea's bedroom with the lot of you!"

"Put a lock on that door, Bill. And let me help you with that scratch on your forehead." Cathy stated.

"Thanks, and you can count on the lock, honey."

An hour later the four girls were still awake, and a calmer but still visibly shaken Vicky was starting to tell her tale of being in the attic.

"Gaea, I don't think that was a cat that scratched me. I saw a girl and she was like us. I mean our age. But I don't think she is alive."

Bob Pepper pushed his new aspiring writer toward the center of the room. "Jack, my boy, welcome! This day is for you!" The large boss said, smiling broadly. "Today, Pepper and Pepper Publishing has discovered a new star! I present to you all Jack William Jefferson!"

The people in the room exploded in cheers, atta boys, and laughter. Jack stood stunned, trying to take it all in. His novel was being displayed on a large screen. He recognized the title and his name, yet not the artwork. A bishop adorned in red robes seemed to be leading a procession of priests down a stone passageway, steps that led into darkness; the only light was from handheld torches that flickered against the damp walls that he assumed led to catacombs. One of the dark places that he created in his mind.

"I don't understand."

"Jack, you're fired," Pepper said with a wide grin.

"Bob," Mary said, looking leerily at her boss. "That's not fair."

"Okay, okay then. Fired and rehired. Maybe I should say promoted. Either way, Jack, you are the new addition to the growing list of Pepper and Pepper authors! And if I am correct, and I usually am spot on with these decisions, you will be our new best-selling author within this quarter!"

The room exploded once again in applause. Jack sat on the closest chair he could find; his mind spinning. "What does this mean, sir?" He asked, looking up at his boss.

"It means, my boy, that I enjoyed your manuscript and read it three times. Not to make up my mind, I just loved your storytelling and how you wove the suspense and horror together. You are going to keep people up at night reading. And perhaps they will be checking their closets and under the bed before trying to go to sleep. That, Jack, is a formula for success." Pepper nodded to his secretary.

Dottie produced a blue hard-back folder inlaid with Pepper & Pepper Publishing and embellished in gold gilt. He noticed it was scripted in a beautiful cursive Edwardian font. She laid it down in front of Jack.

"Open it. It is the, how do authors put it? Oh yes, the door to your future." Bob Pepper said, smiling broadly.

Jack ran his hand over the jacket. He could feel how the writing had been pressed into the folder's material. He opened it and looked at the contract that was presented. An envelope, equally ornate as the folder, was attached to the contract with a gold paper clip.

"Cliff?" Bob said. "You better take it from here."

The company lawyer came forward, sat beside the young author, and extended his hand. Jack shook it weakly. "Hello, Mr. Harford," he said. As the company runner, Jack had been to Cliff Harford's office picking up or delivering documents. He had never given much thought to a lawyer's job in a publishing company. Now, he was getting a crash course about how it pertained to himself as a new writer.

"I would say welcome aboard, but that is hardly needed. Congratulations is more like it. On this promotion, if you will." Harford said.

"This is a contract."

"It surely is. I am here to answer any questions you might have. It is quite standard. In the envelope is the consideration offer that Pepper and Pepper is making to you in exchange for the rights to publish your work, promote it, and other costs they might incur while making you a literary star. After that check, your first novel's royalties will determine how much money you make, and of course, that is based upon sales. I think you will find the amount more than sufficient to cover your expenses until you begin earning royalties and author your next book."

Jack pulled the envelope from the folder and turned it over in his hands. "I have five more." He said softly.

"What was that, Jack?" Bob asked.

He looked up. "I said, I have five more manuscripts. All of them sequels to this one."

Bob Pepper nearly fell on the floor but composed himself. His own mind began to race. Five more manuscripts are written and ready for edit. Based on this masterpiece. The lad had already written his ticket for the next decade, and if Pepper's intuition were on the spot, this would ensure the company's success for years to come. Even Bill Pender didn't crank out work like this kid. The boss cleared his throat and looked at Harford.

The lawyer turned his attention back to the business at hand as Jack removed the check from the envelope. It was Jack's turn to smile as he read the amount on the check. "So much."

"Standard amount plus more. The publisher has the option to offer monies they deem equal to their author's talent. As I said, the contract is standard as well. Feel free to read it. Oh, it's not that thick, as there are three copies. One for you, one for the publisher, and one I must file. Legal bullshit, and all that." The crowd in attendance laughed at the remark.

An hour later, champagne glasses had been filled more than once. Jack was quickly becoming many of the people in the room's new best friend, and the taste of the fame that might be coming was already starting to wear on him. Thankfully, Bob Pepper brought the celebration to a close.

"That's a wrap, folks. Everyone have a great weekend!" As the employees began to leave, Pepper pulled his new author aside. "Jack, your book is already being pressed and copies will be hitting the shelves very soon. I need you to get whatever you need to do in order. Your days of running around this factory are over. I'm sending you to Maine shortly."

"Maine?"

"You bet. You are going to do a book signing in New England."

"But why Maine?"

"Because you are going to be the guest of, and do a signing with, Bill Pender."

CHAPTER 13
A New Addition

"And here we are!" Laurie said cheerfully, hopping out of the car and opening the door for her passengers. "Welcome to Shaw Manor!" Dr. Tarpon climbed out and stretched. Mary Van Buren followed, and the two gazed at the house together.

"Quite impressive," Jeffrey stated. "When they said a manor, that was no understatement."

"Quite. Pay the girl, doctor."

"Oh yes." He replied, reaching for his wallet.

"They are here," Cathy called upstairs to her husband.

Bill leaned back in his chair and sighed. "I wonder if this room was your dreamer's hideaway, Captain Shaw." He reached forward, turned off the computer screen, and looked out at the Atlantic Ocean through the French doors of the widow's watch. "But of course, your paradise was the sea. Isn't it such for every true sailor?"

"Coming!" Bill called back.

As Tarpon paid Laurie, a police car pulled up beside the cab. Cathy appeared at the front door, followed by Bill a moment later. "Why is there a cop here?" He asked.

"No idea," Cathy replied.

"That's Chief Jackson." Bill stated." Who is that with him?"

"My god, Bill, it's Victoria." The police chief stepped out of his car, followed by a woman who opened the rear door for the young girl.

"What the hell? Cathy, you greet our expected guests; I'll talk to Craig and see what happens with Gaea's friend."

"Good morning! You must be Mrs. Pender. I hope we have not arrived at troubled time." Tarpon said glancing at the police officer.

"Neither Bill nor I have any idea what that is about. But I think my husband is about to find out." Cathy assured him.

"May I present my colleague Dr. Mary Van Buren? I am Dr. Jeffrey Tarpon. I must thank you for your gracious hospitality in helping us with our research."

"I am an antiquities scholar," Cathy said, grasping the outstretched hand of Tarpon and then Dr. Van Buren's. "Anything for furtherance of science."

"Excellent," Mary added. "Doctor Catherine Pender. I have read your papers in your field. I especially found *Antiquities and Relics of the Norsemen of a Maine Settlement* quite fascinating. I would be quite interested in chatting with you about your findings and hypotheses."

The trio was interrupted by Bill. "Cathy, can you come here for a moment please?" He waved to the scientists and smiled. She excused herself and walked to her husband. She could see Vicky and that she had been crying. The girl stood partially behind the woman clutching a doll. Her light blue dress danced gently in the ocean breeze.

"Honey, we have a significant issue here. This is Mrs. Pamela Sevigny. She works for the county as a child caseworker. Chief Jackson and Victoria, you already know. Can you take them into the house? I'm going to show our other guests how to find the Shaw family cemetery. It will give us time to figure out what to do with this problem." Bill informed her.

"What is the problem?" She asked.

"You will know very shortly. Please, go inside. Let Victoria go up to Gaea. Then the four of us can talk, OK?"

"Vicky." The girl said softly.

"Of course, Vicky," Cathy said, taking the girl's hand. "Let's go see Gaea."

Bill showed the pair of researchers the path to the cemetery, promising a tour of the house later. He ensured full access to the widow's watch library, less his personal works and computer. The two doctors eagerly agreed and charged up the path along the stone wall. Bill turned and headed back to the manor, shaking his head. There was more to worry about than scientific discovery. A young girl's future was at stake.

In the widow's watch, unbeknownst to anyone, a statue sat in the corner, eyes glowing red.

It took Jack Jefferson all of five minutes to clean out his employee locker and carry the box up to the creative wing of Pepper & Pepper to his new temporary office. The space was large, and being on one of the upper floors of the building afforded a magnificent view of the city. Granted, it was not as elaborate as Robert Pepper's, but it was a vast improvement from his locker in the employee lunchroom.

He dropped the box onto his new desk. A new Apple computer dominated the mostly empty space except for an old Royal typewriter and two reams of paper. Jack smiled. His publisher had remembered that he preferred to write on an older machine. He had no fondness for new gadgets, although a new mobile phone would probably be needed. Carrying around a pocket full of change to use a pay phone, which was rapidly disappearing, seemed inane. His beeper would have to be replaced.

Jack sat in his new luxurious chair and put his feet on the desk. He looked around the office at the empty walls, a blank piece of paper waiting to be written on. Such was a writer's mind. Full of scrambled thoughts and words waiting to be organized into sane ideas that would become a tale, a story, or perhaps even an epic telling of chivalry. Jack laughed.

"This is not you, Jack." He thought. Perhaps going to visit the best-selling author was a promising idea. From what he knew of Bill Pender, he was a very down-to-earth individual and loved his privacy. There was much to learn from a person such as him. Jack was an expert when it came to research, and it was time to dig into the man who might become a mentor. The phone on his desk beeped, and he noticed it for the first time. Lights were flashing all over the device, and he had no idea what any of them did.

"Hello?"

"Sir, Mr. Pepper, on line one." A female voice came through the speaker.

"What? What does that mean?"

"Press the button labeled number 1, sir."

"Thank you." Sitting up, he pressed the button. "This is Jack."

"Pepper here. How are you settling in?"

"It's not really me, sir."

"No more, sir, Jack. And that office is only temporary, or for as long as you want it. Let you get settled in, so to speak."

"Who was the woman that called me?"

"That would be Diane. She is an intern and, for now, your secretary."

"I don't want a secretary." He protested.

"Jack, again, it is only temporary. Things are to be done as we publish you and introduce our new star to the world. You might not need her, but I do. Itineraries, for example. You are about to become a busy man. Don't make me have to track you down like Bill Pender. That guy drives me batshit."

"I was just about to head out and go buy a cell phone," Jack replied.

"Excellent. Get a good one, not one of those cheap pieces of crap."

"I will, sir."

"Stop saying, sir, Jack." Pepper reiterated and then hung up.

Bill entered the manor. Cathy had chosen the dining room for the impromptu meeting, and he smiled as he joined them. "Where is she?" He asked.

"Upstairs with Gaea, Bill," Cathy answered. "All good with the scientists?"

"You bet. No worries about them. It seems we have a big one here. Have you been filled in, babe?"

"Yeah, and it's not good. It seems Victoria is now an orphan."

The caseworker laid a file on the table and opened it.

"Her father was killed in an accident last night. We are waiting for the toxicology report, but preliminarily, it seems alcohol intoxication." The Chief added. "There was a bottle of Jack on the seat of his truck."

"According to records, yesterday was the anniversary of his wife's death." The caseworker added.

Bill leaned back in his chair and rubbed his hands over his face. "So, what are her options?"

"She screamed, Bill," Cathy said, grabbing her husband's hand. "When she found out. She has no family."

"That is correct." Mrs. Sevigny said. "We have no place to take her, and she would not stop screaming your daughter's name. We have no placement for her; she needs a temporary foster home. Unless we send her out of state."

"That is not going to happen, Bill. I will not see a young girl shipped out because no one cares for her." Cathy said angrily.

Bill sighed and thought for a moment. "I met her father here at the manor for Gaea's birthday. He was nice but seemed off somehow."

"He abused her," Cathy said, staring at her husband.

"What?"

"According to police records, we have reports of complaints against her father. Nothing was done."

"We tried to follow up on those." The chief said. "She never cooperated. Sometimes I feel helpless."

"It's not your fault Chief Jackson." Pam Sevigny said. "Children become so afraid that they fear the repercussions of even their own mother or father."

"Monstrous," Cathy said.

"So, what do you want from my family?" Bill asked.

"Foster her until we can find a proper home," Pam said, sounding hopeful.

"It's a lot to ask," Bill replied.

Cathy stood up and nearly slapped her husband's face. "If you do not agree to this you can sleep up in the watch for the rest of the year!"

He raised his hands in surrender. "Cathy, of course we will. I am more concerned about her mental health. She just went through a traumatic event."

"Mr. Pender, issues such as that are covered. Anytime Victoria needs psychological help, regular checks will be done by me or my staff. We are here when she needs it. I think what she needs right now is a friend like your daughter and a loving home."

Cathy glared at her husband.

"What? I'm not the baddie here. You know I am always the good guy. Who gave you the napkin ring and asked you to marry me?" The chief and Pam laughed.

"He did," Cathy said. "Over at the Cliff House."

"Where do we sign?" Bill said.

Cathy stood up. "I will go get the girls. It's a huge day for Victoria."

"Vicky." Bill reminded. Cathy leaned forward and kissed her husband.

CHAPTER 14
A Morbid Discovery

Vicky could not be happier. She had a new home, even if temporary, and her best friend would be there for her. Even as Gaea led her to her new room, she looked at the attic door; seeing the padlock on it gave her peace. Terror lay in wait in such places. She despised attics, and if she never set foot into another one, that would be a blessing. Being with her best friend at the Shaw Manor filled her heart with joy. Vicky had loved her father, but the alcohol and abuse he doled out was unbearable. When she learned of the accident and his death, she cried; then relief and Gaea came into her mind. Her savior had always been Gaea. She was smart and beautiful and gave Vicky the care she desperately craved. It was because of Gaea that she chose to take the name Vicky. Her father, when drunk and angry, scolded her for using Victoria, and she hated it.

When people came to take her away, she screamed until they listened to what she was trying to say. It was Chief Jackson who recognized that it was Gaea and the Penders that she was crying for. After a brief discussion with Pam, the girl's immediate fate was decided. Take her to Shaw Manor and hope for the best. Of course, the courts would be involved in the near future, but if the Penders decided to help, life would become much easier for Vicky. They took her to the hospital for a checkup. After a clean bill of health and paperwork, Vicky was released to the custody of the county's representative, Pam Sevigny, and was on her way to what could become her new family.

She loved the Penders. Who would not want them? Vicky had never really experienced having a mother. When she was at Shaw Manor and watched how Gaea and her mother interacted, it made her heart ache. Sometimes, people were so lucky.

Piddles waddled up to her and sat down, her stub of a tail wagging fiercely. She reached down and scratched the puppy behind its ears. "I'm happy here, too," Vicky said quietly to the dog.

Finding the Shaw Cemetery was easier than Dr. Tarpon had thought it would be. The narrow path that led along the property was separated by a sheer cliff that dropped to the Atlantic by an aging stone wall and the dense Maine woods to the west. Luckily, the Penders had seen fit to have the path kept cleared and clean of debris. After a short walk, the scientists arrived at a fenced-in plot cut neatly into the foliage. The same stone wall surrounded its perimeter except for the entrance. A wrought iron gate stood before them; the name SHAW welded ornately in an arch at its top. No rust was to be seen anywhere on the metal, and the black paint looked fresh. Another thing the Penders seemed to be taking care of. It seemed that the Shaws were being fondly remembered by the manor's new caretakers.

"Shall we go in?" Mary asked. "Or are we going to admire the gate for the next decade?"

Tarpon smiled and pushed the heavy gate. It opened effortlessly with nary a screech nor a squeal on well-oiled hinges. The duo entered and took in the simple surroundings. Two large headstones expertly crafted from granite stood at the west end of the plot, seemingly keeping watch out to sea. They approached, and Tarpon ran his hand over the polished stone. Van Buren dug into her satchel and retrieved a roll of Pellon and a large block of charcoal.

"Are you sure we should take a rubbing without permission, Mary?"

"I don't see why not. We were granted permission to do research here. Rubbings don't harm the stone, Dr. Tarpon."

"Of course not. Perhaps I am being oversensitive and cautious."

Mary placed the paper over Lily's stone and started to rub the etchings into the paper. "Look through the rest of the plot, Jeff. Maybe there is an artifact or two hidden somewhere."

"I should have brought the metal detector." He said, standing up.

Vicky hugged Cathy with all the strength in her young body. "Please don't take me away Mrs. Sevigny. I don't want to go to Mass-shutes!"

"Massachusetts." Gaea corrected, sitting next to her friend.

"I don't care what it's called. I want to stay here!"

"Shh," Cathy whispered, caressing Vicky's hair. "You are not going anywhere. Not if Bill and I have anything to say about it. Right Bill?"

"Of course, honey." He replied and thought, "Pender's Shaw Manor is about to become an orphanage. I wonder if Lily would have approved."

"Victoria?" Mrs. Sevigny asked quietly.

"Vicky." The girl answered.

"Of course, Vicky. I need to ask you a few questions. Would that be ok?"

"Yes."

Chief Jackson leaned over and whispered into Bill's ear. "I wish we could go to the other room for a drink. Can't. I have to be the witness. I hate this kind of shit." Bill nodded and turned his attention back to Vicky and the caseworker.

"Vicky, how well do you know the Penders?"

"Gaea is my best friend!"

"Yes, but how well do you know the family? Have you been here a great deal?"

"She has." Gaea broke in. "Lots. She was here for my birthday party and a sleepover."

Cathy looked at her daughter, and Bill grasped his wife's thigh under the table. Bill had an idea where this was heading and gave his wife a look. "I think Vicky needs to answer, Gaea." He told his daughter.

"Oh, I've been here lots. Gaea helps me with my schoolwork and lots of other stuff." Vicky affirmed.

"That's nice." The social worker said, scribbling notes into Vicky's file. "And have you ever felt afraid here?"

It was Gaea's turn to grab Vicky's leg and give her a look.

"Oh, no, never."

Bill sighed and leaned back in his chair.

"Have you ever been threatened by any member of the Pender family?"

"No," Vicky said as Chimer jumped up onto her lap. "See, even the cat likes me. And I love him, too." Two hours later, the questions continued.

"Mary, come take a look at this."

The scientist was finishing placing her new scrubbings into evidence bags and stood up. Behind her, Jeffrey Tarpon was using a brush to complete the shallow excavation he had just dug. Standing over her colleague, she looked down at his work. "Another one?"

"It seems so. I tripped on the corner of it. It's a flat stone, and it's sinking into the earth. Look, there is an engraving." Brushing more soil away, a name was revealed. *Rebecca MaryAnn Shaw.* "Another family member," Tarpon said. "But I think there is even more."

As the dirt was pushed away, the relief of a cross was revealed, and an angel lay over it, appearing to mourn the loss of the soul buried in the dirt beneath, its wings broken in sorrow.

"My God." Dr. Van Buren said. "It's the grave of a child. How incredibly sad."

He looked up. "I think it's time to visit the Shaw library."

"I'm sorry that was so brutal." Pamela Sevigny said closing the file and placing it into her briefcase. "I don't make the rules, but I do have to follow them. However, Victoria Lauren Walsh is now in the custody of your family until an adoption is ratified if you so desire. The paperwork is there in the folder with the other documents that you signed. I'm afraid the waiting period before you can file an adoption request can be up to a year, and during that time, I, or another caseworker, will have to come and review her living environment."

"Bill, I have a couple of suitcases of that girl's in my trunk." Chief Jackson said. "She didn't have much, but I'll go fetch them."

"I'm staying?" Vicky asked excitedly.

"Welcome to our home," Bill said, hugging her. "Come on, let's take you upstairs. Gaea, can you help her settle into her new room?"

Cathy smiled broadly as her daughter took her friend's hand and watched as the two skipped out of the dining room. Cathy embraced her husband and kissed him. "I love you."

"I love you too. But the next child you want might have to wait."

"Don't be so sure." She said, rubbing her tummy.

CHAPTER 15
Departures & Arrivals

"We're back!" Clarissa called from the front door. Followed by her husband, the two entered the foyer. "Hello?" Doug called out.

"Hey there," Cathy said, entering the great room.

"What was up with the cop car?"

"Long story," Bill answered. "You two have a good day?"

"Great!" Doug chimed in. "Shopping and a wonderful lunch at this little place called The Ogunquit Square. It was the first time I had braised sea scallops in a white wine sauce. And the wine…"

"Spectacular. But we need to pack and leave." Clarissa interrupted. "It seems Bob has a new genius writer, and I need to meet the man. You know how demanding Robert Pepper can be."

Bill laughed. "Better than most. I pity you, but hey, it could turn into a great client, Clair. Bob has a knack for finding extraordinary talent."

"It had better! I need more than one Bill Pender to fund my husband's new golfing habit."

"Oh, shush, honey. I hardly play. I'm too busy catering to my beautiful wife and her extravagant desires."

Cathy laughed along with Bill. "She makes more money than you, Doug." Bill chuckled.

"Don't remind me. It's how I became her indentured servant."

"Would you two Cro-Magnon's shut it?" Clarissa moaned while rolling her eyes.

"I second that motion," Cathy said.

"Well, you both know you are welcome here anytime. Gosh, you know we have the room."

"Oh, a couple of weird-looking people are coming out of your woods. Ground maintenance?" Doug said, pointing out the window.

"No. There are two scientists here to research the Shaw Manor."

"We'd best get packed then and get out of your hair. Our cab will be here soon, and we have a plane to catch over in Sanford."

"It must be important if Bob is sending the corporate jet."

"Who mentioned corporate?" Clarissa asked.

"Clair, Sanford does not have a resident airline," Bill responded with a chuckle.

"Fine. I told you I needed STAT."

Bill grinned. "Enjoy your flight."

As the couple ran up the grand staircase, the bell rang at the front door. Bill rolled his eyes and walked to greet the next set of guests. He was greeted by two very striking people. He had not had the opportunity to look at them properly when they had initially arrived. A man of tall stature stood before him dressed in khaki, as Bill would have expected a scientist to be in the field. His associate was also dressed in a well-pressed khaki uniform, sporting the Archaean Horizon logo above their left breast pocket and their names stitched neatly over the right.

"Hello," Bill said grasping the outstretched hand of the woman. "Bill Pender."

"Dr. Mary Van Buren." She replied with a smile. "This is my colleague Dr. Jeffery Tarpon and the head of our expeditionary team aboard the Archaean Horizon."

"Very nice to meet you, Mr. Pender." Tarpon shook his hand firmly.

"Come on in. And it's Bill. I hate that formal stuff."

"Very well, Bill, it shall be. You can call me Jeff, and this is Mary. We have some startling news you and your wife might be interested in."

"Ah, the discovery of the Constance. Cathy told me."

"More than that," Mary said. "Before we sit together, can we take a look at the library?"

"Yes, Dr. Van Buren. I believe that would be prudent. It should not take long, Bill." Tarpon said, nodding his head.

Cathy appeared from the kitchen, followed by the two girls. Both were holding onto sandwiches. "Hi! Welcome to Shaw Manor!" she said, walking quickly to re-greet the two. The girls tagged along, chewing, whispering, and giggling with one another.

"Ah, Mrs. Pender," Mary said. "How nice to see you again. And who do we have here?"

"This is our daughter Gaea and her friend Vicky."

"I don't believe I have ever laid eyes upon two more beautiful girls in my life."

"I agree, Jeff."

"Might I ask a question?" Tarpon asked, looking at the two girls. "I know where the exemplary name Victoria is from. Such a powerful queen had the name and ruled England for quite a time. Did you know that my dear?" Vicky shook her head. Tarpon smiled. "Now, Gaea is quite extraordinary as well. One of your parents has an interest in ancient Greek mythology."

"That would be Cathy," Bill said.

"Do you know what your name means, Gaea?" The girl shook her.

"I never thought of telling her," Cathy answered.

"May I?" The scientist asked.

"I guess it would be ok." She looked at her husband. "Bill?" He nodded his assent.

"Well. Gaea is an incredibly special and beautiful name. It means the 'Mother of the Earth'."

"But I'm only ten and don't even like boys."

"You said you liked Brian," Vicky said.

Gaea glared at her friend. "Mom, can we go back and finish our lunch?"

"Of course, you can." Cathy smiled and quickly led the girls toward the kitchen.

"Sometimes Jeffrey has the tact of a sea urchin," Mary said.

"I meant no offense. I have never encountered anyone with that name. I'm a scholar of Greek mythology."

"None taken, I'm sure. My daughter is very gifted for her age. She will start with the questions and luckily, I have an intelligent and patient wife. Now, how about I take you to the widow's watch." Bill said, starting to move in the direction of the grand staircase.

"Widow's watch? Ah. The library. It makes sense that the library would be Captain Shaw's personal space." Mary said.

"And a special place for his wife to watch for him to return from the sea," Tarpon added. "Lead the way, Mr. Pender."

Dr. Roland Brambilla was busy with what he did best: meticulously examining and cataloging artifacts that were being brought up from the ocean floor. The wreck of the Constance was supplying a plethora of archeological gold. The anchor was resting in its nitric acid bath, and it would take time and work for the preservation to be complete. Dr. Tarpon had seen to it that the Archaean Horizon's labs had been equipped with ultrasonic baths, of which all were in use, conserving the dozens of smaller objects that the divers were retrieving. Among the items were three that had drawn his attention more than the others. A pocket watch that seemed of fine artisanship was now being treated. No crew member from the time of Constance would be able to afford such a piece and, the scientist surmised, would not wear it during a fishing expedition. Only the captain would own such an item. A pocket watch would be invaluable to running his ship. He hypothesized that the watch must have belonged to Captain Shaw.

A glass eyeball was also recovered from the site. In the early 1800's, glass eyes were being imported from Germany and being used mostly in and around Virginia. The prosthetic was fit by a local oculist who had become the modern-day ophthalmologist. More often than not, the glass eyeballs did not fit well, as they were not custom fit to the patient. The stock glass eyes were used after surgery, and most individuals eventually opted for an eye patch. It struck Brambilla that a fisherman would choose a prosthetic over a patch, considering the nature of his work.

The last item that completely astounded him was the discovery of a small strong box. He could not fathom why a fishing schooner would need a strong box on board. Common sense dictated that the ship's logs would be taken by the captain after each voyage, especially if the skipper was the owner of the boat. Unfortunately, the old strong box was not waterproof, so anything that it held was more than likely destroyed by the salty waters of the Atlantic. Opening the strong box was on hold until his colleagues returned from their side expedition to the Shaw Estate. Hopefully, they would uncover information and more answers.

The night before Tarpon left for the mainland, the two had laid in bed and talked well into the night. They had agreed that when they co-wrote the journal article on the discovery of Constance, they would include Mary Van Buren as well. Her research needed to be included, and she deserved to be a co-writer of the article.

Their discussion then turned to what to do with the site and the relics that had been retrieved. The wreck site was an easy decision. It would be cataloged and chosen as an underwater grave for the men who perished on the boat. They would have a diver place a plaque at the site listing the names of the captain and crew if the Constance manifest could be found. They had an intern acquiring one from local sources in the town of York, Maine.

When it came to the artifacts, a debate ensued. A local conservatory, such as a museum, was mentioned. Roli brought up the possibility of the Smithsonian in Washington. That idea was quickly scrapped. The Constance was of interest to New England and not the nation. The obvious was finally chosen. All the items would be sent to the Maine Maritime Museum in Bath, Maine. It was the only choice that made sense.

All but a few books in the Widow's Watch library were Bill Pender's personal collection. The broken windows and destroyed French doors had let the elements in and destroyed what had probably been a treasure trove of volumes that Captain Shaw had acquired, except for one top shelf at the rear of the room.

"Jeffrey, look here," Mary said, pointing up at the older books.

He counted eleven books on the shelf, all similar in thickness and bound in leather. Next to them was a large and thick book with the words Family Bible engraved in gold guilt on its spine. Carefully, he removed one of the books that was bound in leather. It was old but seemed to be in excellent condition. He turned it over in his hands and read the inscription etched on its cover. *Fishing Schooner Constance Deck Log, Captain Wilbur Herbert Shaw, 1870.* Tarpon looked wide-eyed at Mary. "I think we hit the jackpot."

"Open it."

He carried the log to Bill's desk and gently laid it down. Opening the cover, he was greeted with an astonishingly well-preserved document. The captain had taken great care in preparing and writing his notations. Tarpon read the text on the first page.

"Tomorrow, the Constance sails on her maiden voyage with me as her captain. I have assembled what I believe to be a fine crew of good stature. All are God-fearing men who are needed to fair well on the Atlantic in the Gulf of Maine. We fish for salt cod as it is in high demand at the ports and will bring more than a good price. The crew has been promised a fair share of the catch, and I will honor the agreement. I pray for fair weather and the wind to fill my sails as I put forth to the sea. May God grant me His blessing to fill my holds and bring my crew home safely."

The page was neatly signed by Captain Shaw and dated September 2, 1870.

The following pages held cargo amounts, monies earned, monies paid, and simple notations from the skipper concerning fishing areas along the Gulf of Maine. They also included weather and hap stances that concerned the crew, including injuries. One such entry detailed a crew member losing his left eye to the barb of a hook.

"The Constance maiden voyage under our captain. Do you think all the volumes on the shelf are like this?" Mary asked.

"I would bet they are. And if they are in chronological order, we have a complete history of our boat. Except, I would think the year of her demise"

"What about the Bible?" Dr. Van Buren inquired.

"Let's take a look."

CHAPTER 16
Jack Rabbit & Revelations

"Honey!" Bill yelled, coming into the manor. "Cathy, where are you?"

"In the kitchen cleaning up." She called back. Bill stormed in and sat down heavily at the bar, clearly upset. His wife turned, drying her hands with a dish towel. "What's wrong, babe?"

"Bob again. He set me up with another book signing and appearance. And it's a big venue."

"So, you know you must attend those. It promotes your work."

"It's not that. He is sending that new kid here to join me for the event. Bob thinks it will be good for his career."

"How cool is that, Bill!" Cathy exclaimed, excited for her husband.

"Bob wants us to have him here. At the manor."

"That's okay. We have room."

"OK then, I am having a new sign made that will read Pender's Bed & Breakfast and Orphanage at Historic Shaw Manor and Estate. You can run the nursery."

Cathy laughed as her husband started to loosen up. "C'mon, you have been hanging with girls for so long it's becoming pitiful. Live a little. Maybe the boy will be good for you."

He looked up at his wife and smiled. "You are completely insane, Mrs. Pender."

The two scientists walked down the back stairwell, passing through the washroom and pantry, and appeared in the kitchen. "Oh, sorry if we startled you," Tarpon said, "We thought walking through the rest of the manor would be enlightening."

"And it was!" Mary exclaimed. "I was wondering if the house had servant access throughout."

Bill stood up. "The servant stairs have always baffled us as well. As far as we know, the Shaw's never had servants."

"Most manors that were built in the era were constructed on the premise of a large family eventually occupying the house. There is no reason to believe that was not Captain Shaw's intention." Mary said.

"And they never had children," Cathy said sadly.

"Not necessarily." Tarpon countered. "We have discovered evidence to the contrary."

"What?" Bill asked.

"Dr. Van Buren, can you show the Penders the rubbing, please?"

Mary opened her satchel and removed the rolled-up Pellon paper. Carefully, she unrolled it as Bill and Cathy hovered over the charcoal imprint of the gravestone.

"No way," Bill said. Cathy read the dates and started to cry.

"Yes, I am afraid," Tarpon began, "it seems that one Rebecca MaryAnne Shaw was the daughter Captain Shaw never knew he had. According to the dates, and unbeknownst to Lillian, she was pregnant with Captain Shaw's first child. Of course, even after learning of her husband's death at sea, the child was born months later. I'm guessing here, mind you, and I have limited data to go on. I am surmising that Lillian cared for her daughter until she died at an early age. Your daughter's age, to be exact. There were reasons for people dying in that time."

"Cholera, Tuberculosis, and even Polio could have taken not only the child's life but also her mother, Lillian," Mary added. "The mother died young as well."

Bill sighed and sat down. "I do not want my daughter to know this at her age. We are trying to create a happy and healthy home, and digging up old horror stories is not what I or my wife want."

"Vicky has seen her," Gaea said. The young girl had been listening and decided it was time to speak her mind.

"Honey, what are you doing down here?" Her mother asked. "Who did she see?"

"The girl in the attic," Gaea answered matter of factly.

"Really, Robert? Back to Maine? When did I become your babysitter?"

"Clarissa, this kid is the real deal. He is going to make us a fortune, and he needs a literary agent, and you are the best." Bob Pepper said, taking a sip of his tea. "When have I ever…"

"We are not playing *Never Have I Ever* at a slumber party, Mr. Pepper. Who is this kid, and why should I represent him?"

An hour later, Clarissa was convinced and ready to meet the prodigy. Her husband was not going to like that she was going back to Maine so soon, but this was business and money. If Robert Pepper was all in on this new writer, then there was no way she could say no. Her signing of Bill Pender had made her a small fortune and put her on the map, and the cash was still rolling in from the books that he kept cranking out. She now stood for a half dozen well-known authors, and most were doing very well. This guy already had novels written and was waiting in the wings, just begging to be published. His first one was already coming hot off the Pepper & Pepper presses, and if Bob Pepper was behind this author, then so was she.

Cathy had taken Gaea upstairs to talk to Vicky, leaving her husband to finish with the two scientists. Bill was clearly shaken by the news of Shaw's daughter and was terrified to think she might be haunting the attic. He had believed that the house had achieved peace after what had happened over a decade ago. Now he was not so sure. He stood up and went to the cupboard. Taking down a cup, he filled it. "Coffee?" He asked. "I'll have to micro it."

"I'm good," Mary answered.

"Not for me either. I'm on the decaf these days." Tarpon responded.

Bill sat back down and took a sip, his hand clearly shaking. "What else did you find?"

"The logbooks," Mary said.

"And the Shaw family Bible," Tarpon added. "There is nothing special about it, however. No mention of Rebecca Shaw. Quite ordinary." But the logbooks. Bill, you have the entire record of the Constance, Captain Shaw's career, as well as his crew records and more up there. It's a treasure trove of information."

"I found those in a box in the attic. It seems that the space was somewhat spared by Mother Nature. I brought them down, and after the renovation, I put them in the library. I've never gotten around to even opening one of them. They are quite lovely, and as you might guess, I have somewhat of a soft spot for books."

Mary giggled, surprising the two men. The normally stern and focused scientist was laughing, and Tarpon was stunned.

"A world-renowned author has a soft spot for books." She laughed again, finding humor in the statement.

"I...we were wondering if you would allow us to borrow the volumes so we can analyze them properly. The information they contain will further our research into the history of the ship and its captain. As we speak, my team aboard the Archaean Horizon is retrieving relics from the wreck deep in the depths of the Gulf of Maine.”

“My bounty is as boundless as the sea, my love as deep; the more I give to thee, the more I have, for both are infinite.” Bill quoted, setting his cup on the table.

“Shakespeare,” Mary said softly. “*Romeo and Juliet.*”

“What are you going to do with all the artifacts you are collecting?”

“They will be meticulously preserved and cataloged. Our colleague Dr. Roland Brambilla is leading up that effort. We will write a scientific paper on our findings, and once complete, all the items will be donated to the Maine Maritime Museum in Bath. They have promised a part of the museum to show and educate the public on the Constance and other fishermen that have lost their lives to the Atlantic.” Jeff answered.

Bill thought for a moment and said, “Take them.”

Both Jeffrey and Mary sighed deeply in relief. “We will oversee them as the precious items that they are,” Jeff assured him.

“No, you misunderstand me. “Take them; I am donating them for research of the Constance. With your word, they will be donated to the museum. I owe that much to the good captain and his legacy.”

The scientists looked at one another as a sharp crack of thunder shook the kitchen windows. Heavy rain quickly followed, setting the glass panes awash with water.

“Bill?” Cathy called from the landing of the grand stairs. “Can you come, please?”

“If you will excuse me for a moment, I'll take the Bible as well if you wish. Family items such as that were important to a family back then.”

“Of course,” Tarpon said as Bill stood up. “Mary, did we bring acid-free bags?”

"No, just the standard evidence bags."

"That will have to do. Let's head back to the library and collect our specimens."

Bill and Cathy lay in bed discussing what had happened during an exceedingly long day. Outside, the storm raged on as thunder, lightning, and heavy rain pounded the manor. Even though it was late fall, Mother Nature was treating Southern Maine to a strong summer storm. The noise of the thunder had frightened Vicky to the point that she had fled from her own room and was now curled up in bed with Gaea. Every loud crack made her shake.

"Vicky is with Gaea," Cathy said, twirling her finger in her husband's chest hair.

"I heard."

"What do you think?"

"About what?"

"About today, silly," Cathy said, tugging on one of the longer pieces of hair.

"At the Pender asylum for the clinically insane?" He asked, laughing. "The only one that seems to have a clue is Piddles. At least she has figured out where to eat and piss."

"Seriously."

"Well, it seems we have a new daughter, and I already know we are adopting her. There is no debate about that. That version of the Spanish Inquisition that we were subject to by the case worker was a drag, and our house might be haunted again, this time by a nine-year-old who likes to scratch people. Oh, two scientists asleep in our guest rooms seem to have discovered the source of our possible new ghost: Rebecca Maryanne Shaw. A young girl who seems to have been forgotten by time until today. I would say that overall, it was very productive." Bill stopped and took a deep breath before continuing.

"If you are into having your nerves shredded and like being subject to parapsychological horrors for the second time in ten years. I do not want to go through that again, Cathy."

"It will be ok, honey. The scientists will be gone tomorrow as well as the storm. And we have Clarissa and Jack to look forward to."

"That's it. You're in for it." Bill said, laughing as he grabbed the pillow from behind his head, raising it in mock threat. The evening for Cathy and Bill became a pillow fight and tickle fest that ended in lovemaking.

Two doors down, the girls huddled together and listened to the storm rage. The Boxer curled up between them, snoring indifferently.

Dr. Tarpon lay awake, staring at the ceiling, ideas filling his head to the point where he could not sleep.

Dr. Van Buren lay deep in sleep, oblivious to the world, and dreamt of a rabbit with a watch crawling down a hole.

CHAPTER 17
Maine

Clarissa had to cover her mouth when Jack Jefferson entered Pepper's office. His fiery red hair was enough let alone the freckles. He sported a Star Wars tee shirt and a pair of tie-dyed jeans that looked as if they were recovered from a 1960s love-in music festival. A pair of bright pink hi-top P.F. Flyer sneakers was topping off the ensemble.

"May I present your new client? Clair, this is Jack Jefferson."

Jack smiled broadly and reached out to shake Clarissa's hand. "I'm so happy to meet you. I've never met a literary agent before."

"The kid is a nerd." She thought. "But an adorable one."

Jack sat down and crossed his legs. "So, what's the plan?"

Pepper stood up and stuffed a new cigar into his mouth. He walked to the window with his hands behind his back. Clarissa took notice of the ashtray on the publisher's desk, filled with unlit cigars.

"Bob, you've stopped smoking."

The man grunted. "Mostly. You have known me for a long time, Clair. I'm trying to curb it. My cigars are Cuban and dipped in fine scotch whiskey. I have found that I can get by just chewing on them until the flavor of the scotch is gone. Then I take another one. I've lost over fifty pounds."

"Congrats." She said, "Keep it up."

"Well, let's talk business. Jack, we are sending you up to Maine for a book signing in Boston and Portland, as well as other small towns along the way. As you already know, you will be going with

Bill Pender. You may not have many fans at the venues yet; however, I want you to learn from a master."

"But sir, Mr. Pender hates these sorts of things."

"Nevertheless, it is in your contract to promote your work for your benefit as well as mine."

Jack raised his hand. "I have a demand then."

"Well, that is more like it. Shoot." Pepper said.

"I have a friend. Well, more than a friend. He travels with me wherever I go. His name is Jeremy, and I won't go to Maine without him." Jack stated attempting to sound authoritative and sure of himself.

Clarissa rolled her eyes and thought, "Oh, great. A gay author." She could see the demands building in her brain. The last gay writer she represented was nothing short of Liberace. She prayed this one would be easy to please.

"It's not a big deal." He added. "Jer keeps me grounded because I am a little high-strung sometimes."

Pepper harrumphed and sat down heavily. "I don't see a problem with your, ah, friend going along. He can help your agent with some of the coordination of your book signing. Take some of the load off, so to speak. Right, Clair?"

She glared at Pepper. "Bob..."

"Oh yes. I'll give him a call and finalize the arrangements. You don't have to worry. Sign the lad. I'm going to lunch." He said, standing and heading for the door. "Dorothy? I'm taking you to Chez Moi."

"Well," Clarissa said, opening her briefcase and pulling out a stack of papers. "Let's get you on board."

Bill escorted his guests to the front door to bid them goodbye. Both Jeffrey and Mary were overly thankful to their host.

"Simply amazing, Bill. I am still trying to process that we had the opportunity to spend the night at the Shaw Manor. And I can assure you that your contribution to the project is beyond measure."

"Yes," Mary added. "You have no idea how much this means to our team."

"Oh, I think I do."

A cab pulled up, and a very cheery Laurie jumped out and opened the doors. "Hello again!" She called out. "Hi, Mr. Pender!" Bill waved back as he watched them walk to their awaiting ride. He closed the door, and his cell phone rang.

"Pender."

"Bill! Bob here. We have a slight change of plans."

Roli Brambilla was beside himself with excitement. Jeff and Mary were on their way back to the Archaean Horizon and had the logbooks from Constance. All of them, except for the one when she sank. The discovery of the strong box popped into his mind and was now haunting him. It seemed likely that the captain would have such a place to store the records of the boat's activities while at sea. He recalled an old saying: "Prying eyes cost lives." Could the skipper have been that paranoid of his crew or simply just following his own protocols? Perhaps the deck logs would provide some insight. Jeffrey had promised exciting news upon his return.

In the meantime, Dr. Brambilla was filling nearly every waking hour with his strict style of scientific research. Every nook and cranny of each artifact came under his expert eye. When he was a younger undergraduate in Italy, he had rushed through an examination of an amphora that had been recovered from the Mediterranean Sea. He had pronounced it authentic and wrote his first paper on the artifact, only to be humiliated by his peers when it was discovered to be a fake that had been thrown overboard by someone on a tourism boat. Since the incident, he had worked meticulously to not only bury the memory but to build his reputation as a leading archeologist as well. And his efforts had been overly successful. Awards adorned the walls of his office in Milan, and he had been a featured speaker at scientific conferences and symposiums. His association with Dr. Jeffrey Tarpon also helped further his career. He had jumped at the chance to be included as a lead scientist on the Archaean Horizon's latest venture. An intern popped into the lab. "Coffee, sir?" She asked.

"Espresso, please. And keep them coming."

"Right away."

"I can't believe you told them what I saw in the attic," Vicky said. "That was supposed to be a secret."

"I went down to get a couple of cookies for us, and they were talking, so I stopped and listened. You remember that I told you about Mr. and Mrs. Shaw, who used to live here?"

"Yes."

"Well, those two people that were here. They found a girl buried in the cemetery. They had a kid, and she was our age when she died. It freaked my mom out. That's why I said something." Gaea explained.

"What does it mean?"

"It means, my sister, that you have met a ghost, and her name was Rebecca."

Vicky grasped her doll to her chest and looked at Gaea wide-eyed. "Not a very nice one. She tried to hurt me."

"Maybe you scared her?"

"She scared me! I'm still having nightmares!"

Piddles looked at the two girls and cocked her head.

"Well, Dad put a lock on the attic door, so I think it's OK." She said, but doubts filled her mind.

"Gaea, can I ask you something?"

"Sure."

"Do you think your parents would mind if I called them mom and dad? Like you do?"

Gaea smiled broadly. "Of course, you can. I think they would love that. They are your parents now."

Vicky wrapped her arms around her friend's neck and kissed her cheek. "I love being here!" The dog crawled up and began to lick their faces sending the girls into a laughing fit.

Bill hung up and went to find his wife, who was busy washing bed sheets from the guest bedrooms. "We need to hire a maid, " he said, leaning against the frame of the washroom door and looking at Cathy. Every time he came upon her unexpectedly, he marveled at her beauty, and it was a pleasant reminder of why he fell in love and married the woman. He suspected that Captain Shaw had done the same with Lily.

"Nonsense, I like doing the housework. You know that."

"Honey, there are four of us now, and it's a large house. You have a business to run. Maybe having someone come in once or twice a week just to clean the house. You can still pitter around and do stuff."

"Pitter around? Who washes your underwear, Mr. Pender?"

"You do. I just think a little help would be a clever idea, especially now that Victoria is here."

"Vicky." Cathy corrected.

"Right. Vicky."

"Babe, please." He said, walking over and embracing her from behind. "I'll pay for it."

She turned around and poked her finger into his chest. "You bet your ass you will. You make the biggest messes around here."

He feigned innocence. "My apologies, my lady, for being such a slob." Cathy laughed and kissed him.

"Clarissa and Jack should be here tomorrow, and there is a new twist."

"What?" She asked.

"It seems that Jack is bringing his boyfriend along."

"How nice. I love having guests." Bill said, exasperated and somewhat tired of what he felt was the nonstop invasion of his privacy.

"On the bright side, it will be only two guest rooms to make up."

"Two?"

"I would imagine that our two love birds will share a room."

"I would hope they will be discreet. I'm not sure I want our daughters to become savvy about that part of the birds and bees yet."

"I think one already is," Cathy said, looking across the room. Vicky stood in the kitchen looking at the two, holding her doll. "I know what gay is. Gaea told me."

"Wonderful," Bill said quietly, dropping his forehead onto Cathy's shoulder.

"It's no big deal." She continued. "Mom, Dad, can Gaea and I have a cookie?"

"Of course you can, honey. Just give me a minute, OK?" Cathy answered.

"OK." Vicky skipped back into the kitchen.

"What did she just say?" Cathy whispered.

"She asked for a cookie."

"Not that."

"Oh, she called us mom and dad."

Cathy began to tear up. "Amazing. Simply amazing."

"Go give your daughter a couple of cookies," Bill said, smiling.

About the time that the helicopter was touching down on the Archaean Horizon's aft deck with an extremely nervous Dr. Mary Van Buren clutching Tarpon's arm for dear life, the Pepper & Pepper corporate jet was taking off from the Long Island Municipal Airport for its short flight to Maine. On board, Clarissa was thumbing through the upcoming itinerary. It seemed that two more venues had been added, and she was unsure if Bill was aware of the change. He hated doing these book signings; adding more would not make him a happy camper. Quite frankly, it would piss him off, and she would not hear the end of it. Bob had better have taken care of that as well.

Her husband sat beside Clarissa, flipping through a *Field & Stream* magazine. He was more than angry at the prospect of being left behind again. Especially since his honeymoon had been cut short for the third time, and his wife was planning to go back to where they had just left without him. Work or not, he was going along, even if he had to drive alone to join her. Clair had caved in quickly as she wanted him by her side. If Jack could bring his boyfriend, then she was damned sure she would bring her husband. She looked across the aisle. Jack was curled up with Jeremy, and both seemed sound asleep. "How the hell can anyone sleep during take-off?" She thought.

CHAPTER 18
Rebecca

Brambilla, Tarpon, and Van Buren stood together, looking over the Constance artifacts that had not needed to be subjected to a conservation process. All of them had been cleaned with a simple soap solution and returned to an almost pristine state.

"Glass," Roli said. "Everything should be made of sand and silica."

"I'm not so sure an anchor would do so well," Mary said. The trio laughed as Roli showed them the prize item among the bottles.

Mary looked at Jeffrey. "A glass eyeball. I'm aghast."

"And this was recovered from the wreck?" Tarpon asked.

"Yes. Quite unexpected and an extraordinary find."

"More than you think. Have you started looking at the deck logs we brought back?"

"No. I thought that bringing you both up to speed on the advancements in the Archaean Horizon's labs would be more prudent."

Tarpon smiled and walked to another specimen table. The deck logs of the Constance were laid out and individually contained in archival acid-free clear bags. Tarpon picked one up and carefully removed it from the bag before handing it to Roli. "They are not delicate, but we must follow scientific preservation protocols."

"Of course." He said, gently opening the fine leather cover. "Spectacular."

"Our captain is quite elegant in his writing, as you can see. Read the entry on this page." Jeffrey said, pointing to a log entry in the book.

Roli read the long-hand script aloud:

"September 16ᵗʰ, 1870, Deckhand William "Mac" Farthing has suffered a horrific injury and will be held to bunk for the rest of the voyage. The Constance holds are nearly full, and our return to port is imminent. I feel the utmost responsibility for the loss of his right eye as a barbed hook from a loose line has pierced it at no fault of his own, and I fear it cannot be saved. I have no doctor aboard my vessel, so only limited care can be given. If such as it might be, by my word as Captain of the Constance and by the Lord my God, I will do what is right. His share will be increased by a fair percentage taken from my own, and I shall bear any fees for his care. I will set the course for York in the morn holds full or nay. My crew has been and always shall be my concern. Signed this day, Captain Wilbur H. Shaw."

"Incredible." The scientist said, closing the book. "The glass eyeball. Is all of the…"

"Every volume is detailed with data we could only have dreamt of finding." Van Buren broke in. "They hold the complete manifest, and it appears every detail from every voyage that the Constance has taken under the command of Captain Shaw. Complete names of the crew and hand-drawn maps of fishing areas, personal notes, name it. It's the most complete deck log I have ever laid eyes on."

Tarpon nodded in agreement. "Every log is here but one."

"I think I might know where that missing book might be," Brambilla said, looking at his colleagues.

Vicky woke up, stretched, and yawned. Crawling out of bed, she opened the curtains and looked out over the ocean. The water sparkled in the morning sunlight. She made her bed, which she had never done before moving in with the Penders, and gently placed

Sandy between the two pillows. She adjusted the doll's skirt and hair before kissing it lightly on the forehead. "Now, you stay here. Mommy will come back and get you in a bit. You look tired and need some more nap time."

She didn't dress and decided to have breakfast in her nightgown. Singing as she walked into the hall. Shaw Manor's bedrooms were all on the second floor. The master was in the tower directly across from the grand staircase landing. Above the room was the widow's watch, accessible only by the wrought iron staircase within the bedroom. Next to the master was Gaea's, then a maid's room, designed to be used by the manor staff, followed by Vicky's. Guest bedrooms and broom and linen closets continued toward the north on both sides of the hall, ending with the servant's stairs that led down to the pantry, laundry room, and into the kitchen. The attic door was opposite the primary maid's room, now held shut by a steel padlock that Bill had installed after the girls' incident.

Vicky left the room and walked towards Gaea's room; passing the attic door, she noticed that it began to shake, the lock rattling against the wood of the jam. The girl's eyes became wide, and she fell against the wall clutching her nightgown. The rattling became louder, and the lock popped open. Vicky screamed and ran to her room. Sandy's head lay severed from her body on the floor. On the bed, the doll's torso and the bedspread were covered in blood.

Vicky screamed again and ran to Gaea's room, ignoring the attic door that now stood open. Inside she was confronted by her friend hanging by her neck from the ceiling fan, Gaea's eyes black, dripping blood onto the floor. Gaea's head was bent unnaturally, and a bone protruded from the skin, poking through her nightgown at the shoulder.

Vicky screamed and ran to Bill and Cathy's bedroom. The door was shut, and the girl could not open it. She beat on the door with her small hands and slowly fell to the floor, clutching her knees to her chest. She sobbed and stared at the open attic door, shaking in fear. From within, she heard a young girl's voice. "Victoria, come join me. You know you want to."

Pepper & Pepper's jet turned into the wind on final approach and touched down on runway seven of the Sanford Seacoast Regional Airport amid pouring rain. Slowing, the aircraft turned and taxied to what might be considered a terminal. Clarissa considered it a glorified warehouse.

"Every time I fly to Maine, it rains." She said grabbing her purse and carry-on and standing up. Her husband smiled and stood up also. "You would think with runways like this there would be an actual terminal. Honey, be glad we are back in Maine." Clarissa pushed on Jack's knee, and he woke up sleepily. Jeremy followed, stretching. "We're here?"

"Grab your bags; we have a car waiting." The literary agent said, pushing her husband toward the front of the jet. The lone flight attendant was peering out the window, waiting for the airstair to be pushed up to the aircraft. "How can anyone sleep through an entire flight?"

Doug shrugged. "I hope you brought your umbrellas." He said cheerfully. "Mighty wet out there." Jeremy took Jack's hand and the two followed toward the front.

"Thank you, Danny," Clarissa said as the flight attendant opened the door.

"You are so welcome!" The four walked down the stairs into the pouring rain. "Sorry about the stairs. Ours seems to be stuck." He called after the passengers. "Thank you for flying Pepper & Pepper!"

Vicky awoke and screamed. The sun poured in through her windows and it took a moment for her to adjust to the light. She rubbed her eyes and ran to Gaea's room taking a quick look at the attic door. The padlock hung securely, and the door stood still. She charged into her friend's bedroom and jumped onto her bed, waking the sleeping girl.

"Gaea, I had the most horrible dream."

"What?" She asked sleepily, sitting up. "A nightmare?"

"Yes. But it seemed so real." She cried. "There was blood everywhere and you were…"

"I was what?" Gaea asked. Vicky pointed toward the ceiling and began to sob.

The four family members were having their morning breakfast. Bill and Cathy sat at opposite ends, and the two girls in the center sat opposite one another. Vicky poked at her pancake with a fork, and Gaea looked at her friend with concern.

"Ok," Bill said, picking up his napkin and wiping his chin. "Did the cat die or something? What's wrong, girls?"

His wife gave her husband a look and turned to Vicky. "Honey, aren't you hungry this morning?"

"She had a bad dream last night." Gaea offered. "It scared her really bad."

"Oh?" Bill inquired.

Vicky became angry. "It was that bitch in the attic! The one that attacked me! She wanted me to go join her!"

"Victoria!" Cathy scolded.

"Don't call me that!" she said, starting to cry. Standing up, she ran into the great room and sat down on the sofa. Cathy stood up and followed, taking a seat next to the girl.

"Dad, she really is afraid." Gaea confided.

"It was just a nightmare. We all have them." He replied.

"Not like this. It was the same girl that attacked her in the attic. It was Rebecca."

"Baby, we don't know if that was real. It could have been an animal, maybe even Chimer."

"They found Rebecca's grave, didn't they?" His daughter asked, unrelenting.

"Yes, but that doesn't mean anything."

"The captain's ghost was real, wasn't it? And he never got to meet his only daughter, did he?"

"How do you know about Captain Shaw?" Bill was surprised by his daughter's knowledge.

"I have ears and eyes, and I'm not stupid," Gaea answered the look on her dad's face.

"That, my darling, is a fact. You are far from ignorant. Captain Shaw built this house because he wanted a family like we have. I know he liked to fish, and somehow, he died doing it. One of the paintings up on the landing of the stairs is of him and his wife, and there is no girl. And it is close to the one that is in the Cliff House Restaurant."

"He was famous, wasn't he?" Gaea asked.

"I wouldn't call the man famous, but he was very well respected in York, yes."

"No one builds a house like this to live alone in. Daddy, please promise me you will tell me more?"

Bill smiled. "Of course. I was waiting until you were old enough to understand. I guess that time has come. Let me discuss it with your mother, OK?" Gaea sighed and placed her napkin on her plate. "I'm going to ask Vicky if she wants to move into my room with me. Will that be alright?" She asked.

"It's fine with me. It's your personal space and if you want to share it with her, who am I to say no?" She wrapped her arms around his neck and kissed him. "I hope it was just a bad dream." Gaea then let go, and ran to Vicky and her mother, as Bill sat and watched the three women together.

"Shit." He whispered. It had best be just a bad dream.

CHAPTER 19
Tacos, Pie & A Passing

The rain was still falling as the cab turned onto the road that led up to Shaw Manor. Doug sat in the back next to Jack and Jeremy. Both were curled up against the door, fast asleep. He had given the front seat to Clarissa even though she was smaller in stature. An unhappy and cranky wife was not pleasant to be around.

"We're here!" Laurie said cheerfully, opening the door and grabbing an umbrella. "I can't believe you are back so soon!"

Doug smiled weakly as he climbed out of the car. Was there only one cab driver for the entirety of York County, Maine? The girl was sweet but almost too much, bordering on annoying. He opened his wallet and paid her, then reached in and poked Jack, perhaps a bit too hard. They both awoke suddenly and looked around.

"What?" Jeremy asked.

"We're here. Grab your gear." Doug instructed abruptly. Two umbrella trips later, the foursome stood on the porch, and Clarissa rang the bell. Doug watched as the cab disappeared down the drive.

"Is Maine always this shitty?" Jack asked.

"And it's really cold," Jeremy added.

"Be polite. You are about to meet the famous writer, Bill Pender. We are his guests, and he normally doesn't like company. Be nice." Clarissa said as the door opened to a smiling Cathy, who held an arm full of towels. Clarissa leaned forward and kissed her cheek, and her arm brushed against the towels. "Warm!" She exclaimed.

"Just out of the dryer. Welcome to Shaw Manor, home of the Pender Clan." She said, handing out the towels. "Unseasonably cold rain."

As they entered the great room, Jack and Jeremy were wide-eyed. The ceilings rose to nearly a second story and were massive. The windows were impressive unto themselves, and when Jack saw the grand staircase, he was flabbergasted. "This is amazing, " he said, handing his towel to Jeremy. Look at the fireplace. And that grand piano."

"Look at the tapestries, rugs, and paintings," Jeremy said, making a grand sweeping gesture. He was overcome by the beauty of the works of art everywhere, including on the floor.

"Jer, this is beyond amazing," Jack said, looking at the others. "Oh, you must excuse him; he is an antiquity expert, especially rugs and tapestries. He owns a shop in New York."

"Fascinating," Cathy said. "We have a lot in common then."

"We do?" he asked.

Clarissa smiled. "Cathy is a curator of a museum or was. Doctor Pender now has a shop of her own here in York."

Jeremy stood wide-eyed. "Please take me there."

"If we have time, I will." She answered. "Bill is up in the widow's watch and is waiting for you, Clarissa. Doug, you know the drill. Can you take our guests upstairs and find them a room?"

"I don't know." He said coquettishly. "Are you sure you have enough space? The house is so small and all."

Clarissa slapped her husband's arm playfully. "Don't be a jerk."

"Me? I'm simply happy to be back. I can eat more lobster and whole belly fried clams!"

"Go, or you're getting soup."

He kissed his wife. "Come on boys, let's find you two a bunk."

"Bunk?" Jack said softly to Jeremy.

Brambilla led the scientists into one of the ship's labs, which had been designated for preservation using mild acid baths. In a large vat, a strong box sat, the liquid gently flowing around its surfaces. A padlock still held the box closed, although rust was evident and had permeated the iron. "We are trying to save the box," he said, "but I am more interested in its contents."

"The logbook," Tarpon said, nodding his head in agreement.

"Precisely. When you informed me of your discovery of the full volume of Captain Shaw's and the Constance's deck logs I immediately thought of the strong box. It makes sense that he would keep such an important thing in a safe place."

"The preservation solution is not going to help what may be inside." Van Buren added. "It might be destroying whatever paper is in there."

"That is a strong possibility. However, if we don't open it, we shall never know." Roli acknowledged.

"Let's do," Tarpon said. "If the book is in there, and only a fraction of it can be saved, it will still be a momentous find."

The formal dining room was being used once again. Not for a special dinner, but for lack of space as eight people became crowded around the kitchen table. The evening's dinner was tacos that Cathy, Gaea, and Vicky had cooked up, and it was a hit with everyone. Bill had gone as far as to pick up a case of Tecate beer, and the bottle of tequila from the liquor cabinet had come in handy for margaritas, which Cathy and Clarissa were sipping. Jack, Jeremy and the two girls opted for lemonade and were happily crunching away, Vicky carefully picking out the lettuce. "I'm not a rabbit." She said softly.

Bill laughed and stood up. "Another beer, bud?"

"Sure. I'm back on my honeymoon even if my wife is not."

Cathy snorted and nearly coughed up her drink. "I never got a honeymoon. My husband is too cheap."

"Now that is a bold-faced lie," Bill said, returning to the table, sitting down, and placing a bottle in front of Doug. "I have offered more times than I can count. She was always too busy with work."

"Right, and Mr. Best Seller was not busy. But seriously, then our daughter came into our lives…"

"Oh, so blame it on me then!" Gaea exclaimed, shaking her head. "These two are so lame. Ten years and not even one Disney trip. And you call yourselves parents."

Vicky smiled and giggled. "They are the best parents I have ever had."

The room went silent for a moment, and then Jack broke the awkwardness. "I know what you mean, " he said, thumbing at Jeremy. This one is so engrossed in his work he barely has time for me." Jeremy rolled his eyes and reached for another taco. Writers." Cathy held her hand over her mouth and laughed again.

"Well, I have something very special for dessert," Bill said.

"Really," Cathy said.

"Yup, and I am going to get it right now. Hold onto your taste buds."

Cutting the padlock of the strong box made Jeffrey Tarpon wince as the artifact was essentially damaged. Brambilla noticed the worry on his friend's face and laid his hand on his back. "It's the egg and the omelet."

"Nice analogy." Mary Van Buren said. "Can we open the box, please?"

"Not even a creak," Tarpon said as he lifted the lid.

"It's the solution," Roli noted. "The crud and rust have been removed, and it appears the hinges are in good shape."

The three peered into the strong box. The interior was wet as saltwater had seeped into it throughout the decades. It was lined in leather that, although damaged, had held up fairly well. By archeology standards. "Is that bitumen?" Mary asked. "I didn't think it was used here in New England."

"It was, but not for an application such as this. Roli, have you ever come across something similar?" Jeff asked.

"Only on the hulls of wooden ships. What a clever way to attempt to waterproof a box. A natural petroleum tar such as bitumen makes a fine option considering what was available at the time."

"Much better than oil."

"No doubt, Mary. And look at that." Dr. Brambilla agreed. At the bottom of the box, a leather pouch lay as it had been placed years before.

"Bingo," Tarpon said. "Might that be our missing deck log?"

"One way to find out, Jeffrey."

"What is this?" Vicky exclaimed.

"Yum!" Gaea echoed.

Bill had brought out two boxes, and they lay open on the table. The light green filling of each pie was topped with a few gobs of whipped cream and held by a crust made from graham crackers.

"You outdid yourself. Where did you get these?" Clarissa asked. "It's been years since I have had a good key lime pie."

"I had to make a call, and I was lucky enough to find the number of a small shop down in Key West. Lucy's Pie Shack is still open and run by the same woman who started it in the 50s. I was down there a long time ago and stumbled on it. Back then, she and her husband ran it. He is no longer with us, but she and her daughter keep cranking out the pies. She sent me up a box of them."

"Wait," Cathy said, "a box? Just how many of them did you buy?"

Her husband smiled. "Let's just say there is not a lot of room left in the freezer in the garage. I might have to buy a second one."

"This has got to be the best pie I have ever had," Jack said. "What do you think, Jer?"

"Mucho Coolio! Can we take one home, Mr. Pender?" He asked.

"That is exactly the reason I bought so many. I was counting on Clarissa taking two; since Jack and Jeremey are here, that is two more. Then there is the issue of the midnight raiders." Bill said, eyeing his two girls and his wife.

Cathy dropped her fork on her plate and glared at her husband. "I will have you know, Mr. Pender, that I do not raid the refrigerator at any time."

"Well, I know someone is." He smiled. Gaea and Vicky looked at each other and raised their hands. "I knew it," Bill said, "guilty as charged."

"Daddy…" Gaea was interrupted by a loud screech and the sound of breaking wood.

"Doug."

"I'm with you." He answered, and the two charged up the back stairs.

"Mom! That sounded like…" Vicky said, clutching Gaea.

"Stay here," Cathy demanded. "Can you three remain here with the girls?"

"Of course," Clarissa said. Jeremy and Jack nodded and continued eating their pie.

Bill and Doug were greeted by a troubling sight. The attic door was hanging by a single hinge, and the door jamb was shattered. The padlock that Bill had installed to secure the entry to the attic lay on the floor, broken. Claw marks scratched the inside of the door, and blood spattered the walls and the stairs.

"My God." Bill said covering his mouth with his hand.

Cathy turned the corner and ran down the hallway joining the duo. Covering her mouth, she collapsed to the floor. "Chimer..." She cried and began to sob. At the base of the stairs lay the cat, his eyes torn out, the empty sockets oozing a reddish green slimy liquid that matted his fur. The stench of death drifted down from the attic above.

Doug turned, fell to his knees, and vomited on the floor.

CHAPTER 20
A Missing Link

"Carefully, please," Brambilla said.

The archeologists were engaged in the painfully lengthy process of extracting the pouch from the strong box. A mistake could cause the artifact to crumble and disintegrate. If the trio's combined hypothesis was correct, the missing deck log of the Constance was contained within this tar-coated leather pouch and was hopefully somewhat intact. Saltwater was not a friend of preservation, yet the icy water of the deep Atlantic was, especially if not exposed to sunlight. Tarpon grimaced as he gently raised the pouch and moved it to an exam table, placing it into one of two specially prepared baths of equal parts of Alum, Glycerin, and water. One designated for the pouch and the second for its contents.

"I see no signs of teredo worms," Mary said. "It seems the box and the bitumen have at least spared our artifact from that."

"True," Tarpon said, removing his gloves. "Now, let's see if we can open it. Roli?"

"Let Mary have the honor. I believe she has the more stable, delicate hands."

She donned her gloves and investigated the shallow pan at the pouch. It appeared to be well sealed with generous amounts of bitumen.

"Was it dipped in a vat of tar?" Jeffrey asked.

"Looks like it was soaked in it." She said, picking up a scalpel from the table. "Getting this thing open is going to take time if we are to save the pouch."

The Pender family stood together at the southeast corner of the Shaw family cemetery overlooking a small freshly dug grave. Bill had hired a local fence company, and after groveling and a hefty price, the ironworkers had welded, painted, and installed a custom fence that blended in perfectly with the existing one the Shaws had fabricated decades before. Short notice costs.

The team of ironsmiths had done an impeccable job in blending in the old with the new. Where once was a single gate, there were now two. Bill had chosen to divide the plot into a portion that was a third of the original size. As cremation had become the popular choice prior to burial, and he, being a proponent of saving land, decided a small area would suffice for his family. The wrought iron fence matched the original, and the gates were equal in splendor. Scant feet separating them, the Shaw gate was now side by side with an ornate iron piece of artwork that read Pender.

Bill had also paid another local company to have a small granite gravestone carved and installed at the head of the freshly covered hole in the earth. Simply etched into the polished stone, it read Chimer. Cathy held her husband's hand and placed a wildflower on the dirt.

"Babe, he was old." He offered weakly.

"He was murdered, Bill. Didn't you see?"

The two girls had grown tired of the ceremony and wandered onto the Shaw side. Bill and Cathy paid no attention to them and talked quietly together. His wife was clearly upset.

"Bill, how do you explain how we found him? Chimer was butchered. The blood." Cathy stated, shaking off a sudden chill.

"Honey, the contractors are replacing the attic door and reinforcing it until we can figure out what happened."

Cathy glared at her husband with a look that chilled his own blood. He had never seen such anger in the eyes of his wife. Malice that bordered on hatred.

Clarissa and Doug were in the manor, both contemplating their duties as babysitters for Jack and Jeremy. They did not think that accompanying the family to a pet burial was prudent. The boys spent their time eating, napping, or sitting and looking out at the Atlantic Ocean. Unbeknownst to them, back in New York City, Robert Pepper's blood pressure was through the roof, and he was furious

"A damned cat? Please tell me, Dorothy, that my entire company is not being leveraged upon a recluse bestselling author and a gay kid who will probably become another one of the same ilk over a dead pet. The first book signing for Jack is a week away! Everything is set, and I have invested a lot of money in this for both of them! The New York Times people are going to be there for Christ's sake as well as the A-list of the literary community!"

"Bob, here, take this, " she said, handing him a statin pill and a glass of water. I will call Bill Pender."

"Not good enough." He said, pushing the medication aside. "Get the plane back here. We are flying to Maine."

"We?"

"You bet. I want you to go with me, Dottie."

Bob sat heavily into his chair and turned to look out over the Manhattan skyline. "I need the best of the best to be with me. Dorothy, I've never told you this, but without you, I, this company, would not be where we are today. Your input and guidance, I can never... please go with me to Maine." He said, turning back to face his secretary. "You are better at human relations than I am. You are motherly, and I am a troll."

She giggled, holding her hand over her mouth. Although overweight, Bob Pepper was attractive, and she found that an asset to a man. She couldn't care less about fame and money. As a girl from Iowa, she grew up with strong and dominant men. Over the years, she realized that Bob was not close to being the angry, aggressive man he had been made out to be. His bark had no bite once one got to know him. He was a big teddy bear, and she had grown to care for him. Perhaps even love him. Yes, love was on the table when it came to Robert Pepper for Dorothy. She eagerly agreed, and ran to her desk, and grabbed the phone.

Pepper leaned back in his chair. In the past, he would have reached for his cigar box, now missing from his desk. Instead, he picked up the pill, looking at the glass of water. He harrumphed and walked to his liquor cabinet. He poured a short glass of scotch neat and popped the pill into his mouth. He washed it down with a sip of 21-year-old Glenfiddich. He recapped the bottle and placed it back into the cabinet. "Your last vice, Bobby boy." He said quietly. "And it is going to have to go soon as well."

Mary Van Buren positioned the scalpel to begin cutting away at the bitumen. The trio held their breath as the blade cut into the pouch. Air bubbles immediately began to rise to the surface.

"Stop!" Brambilla exclaimed. "Take it out of the bath! There is air inside!"

She dropped the tool, slid her hands underneath, and drew it from the liquid. Carefully, she placed it on the table.

"What the hell?" Tarpon said, bending to look at the tiny slit that his colleague had made in the leather. "That is not possible."

"Open it, Mary." Brambilla handed the scalpel back to her.

Two long hours later, the leather pouch was ready to give up its contents, and it lay open before the three astonished scientists lay the perfectly dry and preserved final deck log of the Constance.

"No one is going to believe this," Mary said. "Our peers will claim us frauds and lunatics if we write about this find. How can a strong box that is filled with salt water not damage or destroy this delicate leather pouch? Can bitumen really stand up to over a hundred and fifty years in the depths of The Gulf of Maine?" Both men shrugged.

"This ancient waterproofing tar seems far better than anyone could have imagined. I think one of us needs to draft a paper on it to back our discovery." Brambilla acknowledged.

"I can do that. But first, I want to send samples of it for analysis." Mary said. "There have been ancient findings of wood from hulls in the Mediterranean that were well preserved using this method. Am I correct about that, Dr. Brambilla?"

"I have personally examined such specimens, but none as pristine as this."

Tarpon nodded. "Astounding. Testing needs to be done. We best include a sample of the leather as well. Perhaps changes due to the pressure at the depth it was at caused a change at a chemical level?"

"It's a hypothesis we can start with. We can't do it here on the Horizon. We need to send it out. Ideas?" Mary asked.

"We can send samples to Boston College, MIT, and New York University for Attenuated Total Reflectance testing. The results from those tests can point us in the next direction. It's going to take time."

"Agreed, Roli. Mary, can you prepare the samples? I will arrange to get them to the mainland."

She nodded. "Let's take a look at our deck log, shall we?"

Vicky screamed, followed by Gaea's own shrieking startling their parents. The girls were standing over the newly discovered grave of Rebecca. Both were hysterical as they looked down at the stone.

"Shit," Bill said as he and Cathy ran to the girls. Cathy pulled Vicky into her bosom, and Bill knelt to hug Gaea, who began beating her father's chest.

"It's your fault." She screamed. "She is real! The bitch is real, and she attacked Vicky and killed Chimer! Why is she in the attic?!"

"Gaea!" Cathy exclaimed at her daughter's profanity.

"Look!" she said, pointing at the gravestone. A red liquid from the angel's eyes seeped and flowed slowly down its face, dripping onto the earth and staining the ground in dark ochre.

"Bill?"

"Let's get out of here."

Twenty minutes later, the girls were with Jeremy and Jack in the great room and were calming down. Vicky dipped her finger into her cup of ice cream and let Piddles lick it off. Cathy and Bill were out of earshot with Clarissa and Doug in the dining room. Cathy was crying angrily. "Bill, you promised me the nightmare was over."

"Honey, how could I know? I thought it was, and the house has been calm for years."

"Why now?" Clarissa broke in. "I was here for the incident with Tracy, and I've been coming back here a lot since. Now, suddenly, this shit begins again. I don't get it."

"I was here as well," Doug said. "It was not pleasant. And the pictures you sent of the manor before the renovation, Bill. Horrific. I still can't believe what happened."

"What was that? Blood?" Cathy asked.

Bill stood up and paced the room, and after a moment, he stopped. "Rust, maybe?"

Cathy rolled her eyes and sank back into her chair. "Don't be an idiot. You know good and damn well what we all saw. The statue was bleeding from its eyes. It's eyes, Bill."

Doug sighed and scratched his head. "Bill, why don't you and I go back for a second look? Just the two of us. I would like to see this for myself."

He nodded and looked at his wife. "I think we should, babe. The girls were out of control. Maybe if Doug and I go back, we can find a reasonable explanation. But that does not explain what happened upstairs in the hall."

"The contractor has sealed the door, right?" Clarissa asked.

Bill nodded. "And our new cleaning service has cleaned up the mess. I told her it was spilled oil. Painters are coming in a couple of days to paint over the blood, er, discolorations on the walls."

"OK, I know of a very renowned medium I can call."

"Witchcraft, Clair?" Doug asked skeptically.

"Some people have certain senses that we don't. There is nothing wrong with bringing in an outside person for an opinion." Clarissa admonished.

"I agree," Cathy said. "And I am going to call the priest that we used before. Anything to protect my children. I don't want to go through what happened years ago."

Jack walked into the dining room, interrupting the conversation. "Hey guys, the girls want to sleep downstairs tonight. You know, in front of the fireplace. They want popcorn and a good movie."

Bill grinned and shook his head. "And who is going to chaperone this endeavor?"

Jack looked at Bill as if the question was inane. "Jer and me. We love Looney Toons. Who else?" The four laughed nervously, and silence filled the room for a moment.

"Ok, go tell the girls," Cathy said. "The sleepover is on." Jack turned and left the room.

"Well, Doug, let's take a walk and have a look at the cemetery. Cathy, can you start getting the goodies ready? I think we all might be camping in the great room tonight." Bill said. "I think there are some sleeping bags in the garage, and what we don't have, we can make do with blankets and pillows."

"I'm going to go and get some pizza. I don't know what will if that doesn't bring some smiles." Clarissa said. "What is the best one nearby?"

"Luigi's over on route one. You can't miss it. It will be packed, and they have a huge slice of pizza on the roof." Bill answered. "Take my pickup. Keys are over the visor, driver's side."

An hour later, Bill and Doug finished examining the cemetery thoroughly and had returned to the manor. They entered using the pantry door, as they had left through it earlier, so as not to upset the girls. Cathy met them in the kitchen. "Well?" She demanded.

"Nothing, babe. Pine needles and maple leaves blow across the grass in the breeze. No ghosts, no spirits, and no blood dripping from an angel's eyes. Nada."

"I know what I saw, Bill. And so do you."

"I know what I think I saw." Bill corrected.

"I wonder." Doug walked over and sat down at the center island of the kitchen. "Could it have been drops of pine pitch? Your woods are full of pine trees. If a drop or two were blown and fell on the statue's face..."

Cathy crossed her arms. "Really? Pine tar?"

"Honey, I've been thinking about it, and I'm not quite sure what I saw. I was concerned with the girls, and they were hysterical. I think I saw the blood, but now I'm not so sure." Bill took a deep breath and continued. "It's a long shot, but sometimes kids freak out about things. They had just found the Shaw girl's grave." He said, trying to soothe his wife.

"Rebecca, yes. We had all just become aware that the girl had lived. Her grave had sunken into the ground, and until those two scientists showed up and discovered it, it probably would have stayed hidden." Cathy said, pouring herself a glass of water.

"Well, it seems likely that the girls heard about the discovery, and it could be that their young minds and imagination took over. When they stumbled upon the girl's grave and read her name, it could have caused panic. Just a drop or two of watery pine sap would be enough to create a terrifying illusion." Doug added.

"I've caught Gaea eavesdropping more than once, and as clever as she is, partial information can be worse than the entire story. You can take that as gospel from a writer who was the one that caught her on more than one occasion." Bill said.

"I think I can make the fake blood thing stick if I can talk to Gaea," Doug said. "I have a degree in psychology."

"If you can, then I know she can convince Vicky, which will calm that down. We still have the issue upstairs." Cathy walked to her husband and took his glass of water, tears welling up in her eyes. "Chimer."

Bill sighed and hugged his wife. "Another unsolved mystery. Maybe the medium can help?" He offered weakly.

The redeeming quality was that the two young girls had been kept away from the carnage upstairs until a cleanup could be done. Excuses were made, and Bill, Doug, and Cathy were able to put things somewhat back into place before they could see what had happened. Cathy had explained that Chimer had simply died, leaving out the gory details. It seemed that the girls had also bought the notion that a trunk had fallen down the stairs and broke the door, killing the cat.

Chimer had been with Cathy before he married her. She had adopted him from a shelter and his given name reflected the genetic condition of his feline eyes. Heterochromia, she had told Bill when he had commented on the white cat. He had to admit he had become quite taken with the animal and, over the years, grew to love him. Bill fully understood what the loss of Chimer was to his wife and his family.

"I would suggest that the girls not be here when the medium and the priest come to visit. It will only bring new fears to the surface, and the trauma has been overwhelming as it stands." Bill said as he went to the bar and took a low-ball glass from a shelf; he opened a bottle of Jim Beam and poured three fingers into the glass. "Join me, Doug? I normally don't, but this has been one hell of a day."

"Sure."

"Ice?"

"Neat."

"I have an idea." Bill began. "Cathy, you're going to have to help on this. "I have that dreaded book signing coming up very soon, and Jack is going with me."

"And Jeremy. Where are you going with this, Bill?"

"Well, how about if I take the girls with me? Jeremy seems to love spending time with the girls, and while Jack and I are tediously signing books, I am sure he can keep them entertained. That will give you and Doug the time to work with the medium and priest and try to find answers. Clarissa is going to have to go with us, obviously, as our representing agent. Trust me, I would rather stay home."

Cathy smiled broadly. "Bill, that's brilliant. You all take off and leave me here with Captain Psychologist and a haunted house that kills pets and God knows what else."

Bill set his drink down and hugged his wife. "Babe, I'm trying to find some kind of solution."

"I know, and I'm sorry, Doug."

"No worries, I kind of like the name Captain Psychologist. It has a nice ring to it." He said, laughing. "Now I just need a costume and a cape." The front door slammed, and Clarissa called out, "Pizza delivery!"

The early evening turned into a fantastic family and friends affair. The furniture had been moved from the front of the fireplace and provided more than enough room for the six sleeping bags, blankets and the two dozen pillows that lay strewn on the floor. Jeremy had brought a couple of movies with him, and everyone was enjoying Hook, a modern take of the tale of Peter Pan. Everything was going great until Clarissa had to get up and answer her phone. A brief conversation later she called Bill into the kitchen and told him the news.

"Bob Pepper and his secretary are arriving tomorrow."

"Why?"

"It seems he has taken a new interest in book signings." She said, shrugging her shoulders. "Especially this one, which happens to include both of his star authors."

"That is ridiculous."

She smiled and leaned forward to whisper in his ear. "He heard about the cat and wants to stay here."

Bill screamed.

CHAPTER 21
Love & Lobster

The flight from Long Island had proven to be uneventful and the limousine that Bob Pepper had hired was on time and awaiting the couple on the tarmac of the Sanford Airport. The nonstop conversation they had delved into resulted in what he might consider a contract, although one with no signatures. A kiss had sufficed, and it had made their pact official. He and Dorothy were a couple, and the printing magnate could not be happier.

His secretary was overjoyed. Her faithful service to Pepper & Pepper, especially Robert, had spanned the better part of her life, and she had grown to love her grumpy boss. Recently, the changes he was making in his own life to better his health had made her proud. She had hated the cigar smoking, and although she tolerated his love for liquor, Dorothy was ecstatic to see him cut down, and now it seemed he had capped the bottle for good. He promised her during the flight that he was done with it.

Bob's physical appearance had changed for the better as well. Taking more incentives in health, the candy machines in the executive wing of the company had been refilled with granola bars and other healthier treats. He was eating salads for lunch, and when he did eat a sandwich, it was tuna, chicken, or turkey and always on whole wheat bread. Hold the mayo. Bob was taking a statin for his high blood pressure, and eggs had become taboo, at least the yokes. Dorothy had made him a delicious pie; the graham cracker crust was filled with a lemon meringue filling that was completely sugar-free. She kept it hidden and allowed him a small sliver of the delicacy once a day. At first, he was furious, but then a doctor's appointment changed his mind about his secretary, and his lifestyle change began, along with his appreciation and love for Dottie.

"We are going to turn onto Shore Road very soon, Mr. Pepper." The driver said.

"Take us down to that cove." He answered.

"Perkins Cove, yes, sir. We will be there shortly."

"Perfect. We can walk the Marginal Way from there, right?"

"Oh, yes, sir. You can walk all the way to Wells Beach if you want to."

Dorothy looked at Bob questioningly. "What are you up to?" He smiled and pulled her close.

"No, no, no, no, no!" Bill said, standing in the foyer.

"Bill, you're acting like a ten-year-old being denied ice cream." His wife said.

"Cathy, you don't know this man. He is the perfect example of an ogre. And he is coming here. Here to my house!"

"Our house." She corrected.

"What are you screaming about, Bill?" Clarissa interrupted, approaching the couple.

"This is your fault." He answered. "Allowing that man to come here."

She laughed. "And I had a choice? We are talking about one of the most powerful men in New York City. It's not like he's the Don of an Italian crime syndicate."

"I'm not so sure."

"Thank goodness Doug took the girls for fudge at the Viking, and they were spared your tantrum." His agent said, pulling him in for a hug. "Look, I spoke to his secretary, who is with him on this trip, and she says the man has changed."

"From what? An ogre to a troll?"

Cathy slapped her husband's arm. "You hush William Pender. If it wasn't for him, we would not have this house and you would still be writing for romance magazines back on the island."

He shrugged. "Ok, you are both right. I think. But we are out of bedrooms, so they have to stay at a hotel. The Shaw & Pender Bed and Breakfast has no occupancy." The two women looked at Bill wide-eyed, and he laughed.

"Clarissa, can you call Doug?" Bill asked.

"Sure, why?"

"I want him to stop by the Lobster Pound and pick up, let's see," Bill said, counting on his fingers. Ten people. Hm, twenty lobsters, along with two pounds of coleslaw, potato salad, and a truckload of dinner rolls. I am not cooking for this mob."

"Honey, that's perfect!" Cathy exclaimed.

"Let's get to it, Robert F. Pepper waits for no one."

"Bobby, what is this place?" Dorothy asked, looking around at the small fishing village. Lobster traps were stacked on the wooden pier. Boats were anchored in the small, protected cove that had the most beautiful backdrop she had ever seen. From where she stood, she could see brightly colored shops painted with care. Artists worked their brushes on canvas, capturing the Atlantic Ocean's beauty as it crashed upon the rocks. A white footbridge spanned from the village across the cove, where lush green lawns led up to large New England-style homes.

He smiled. "I've never been here. It's a lobstering village called Perkin's Cove. Have you ever had Maine lobster, Dottie?"

"Never. And what are those people doing up there?" She asked, pointing to a line of people walking along the top of a rocky cliff.

"I'm assuming that is the Marginal Way. Want to take a walk?"

She nodded, and the two walked hand in hand toward the beginning of the pathway. Twenty minutes into their walk, the pair sat down on a bench overlooking the Gulf of Maine. Below them, salty spray from the Atlantic flew into the air, and along with the thunder of the water crashing on the jagged rocks below, Dorothy felt as though she had been placed into a fairy tale.

"What do you think?" He asked.

She looked up from his chest. "I think it is the most magical place I have ever seen. It's so different from the city."

"You would live here?"

"Of course, I would. It's so peaceful. Is the rest of Maine like this?"

"I'm not sure. I'm a city boy myself. Want to find out?" Robert asked.

"What?"

"I can't just up and sell the company. It means too much to me. But as the doctor says, I need to relax more and get away. I was thinking…"

"Yes?" Dorothy asked, feeling hopeful.

"Well, I can give more control to certain people to help run the company. As I see it, it runs extremely smoothly right now. I guess money helps."

"Robert, what are you saying?"

"I guess what I am saying is that I want somewhere to get away to that both me and my wife would like to go to, you know, to get away and be by ourselves." Bob ventured.

"Robert."

"Dottie, will you marry me?"

Doug sighed in relief when he and the girls arrived at the Lobster Pound, and as he proceeded to try and place the order, he was greeted with a pleasant surprise. "All done, packed, and ready to go!" A red-headed teenage girl informed him. "Mr. Pender called it in!"

Thankfully, Bill had called ahead, prepaid, and requested that it all be ready as a takeout order. With the help of a couple of employees, the entire lot was placed into the rear of the Land Rover next to the five gallons of assorted ice creams and two pounds of fudge Doug had procured from the Viking. It was taking everything he had left of his stamina to keep the girls from picking at the boxes of fudge. If Clarissa really wanted kids as she claimed, God help him.

"Two bedrooms made and ready," Cathy said, plopping down in the kitchen next to her husband. "Clarissa has the dining room ready as well."

"And the attic door?" Bill asked quietly. She fiddled with her fingers and looked at her husband. "Quiet."

"Let's hope it stays that way until the medium and that preacher man can come." Tears welled up in her eyes, and he pulled her in. "I'm sorry, babe."

"It's not your fault. I...I just want my home back."

"I know."

"I want my children safe, Bill. I want us all safe." Cathy said quietly. Bill kissed his wife as the doorbell rang.

He hurried through the great room and into the foyer. He opened the door and was greeted by a man he barely recognized. The woman he did know very well.

"Who is it, Bill?" Cathy called out.

"A woman from Pepper & Pepper and a guy I have never seen before," Bill called back, trying to keep a straight face. "Dorothy, what have you done to my publisher?"

Bob Pepper reached out and pulled him in for a bear hug. Standing back, he smiled broadly. "I would have you please address my fiancé with respect." He said, winking. "It's good to see you, Bill."

"You too, Bob. You look great! You both do. I must say I'm surprised. Engaged. You never cease to amaze me, Mr. Pepper."

"Are you going to invite them in?" Cathy asked, standing in the great room.

"Of course. Come in, come in."

It was immediately clear to Bill that Robert Pepper had lost a vast amount of weight. Where he once had a triple chin, the fat had been reduced to nearly nothing. At over six feet tall, he was no longer the obese man that Bill had once known. Robert Pepper was now a strikingly handsome man who was slightly overweight.

"Bob!" Clarissa exclaimed, hurrying over to give him a hug. "Did my ears just deceive me? Did I hear you are engaged?"

"Bobby proposed on Marginal Way," Dorothy said, hugging her. "It was incredibly romantic."

"Bobby?" Bill asked.

"It's what Dottie calls me." He answered.

"Dottie and Bobby. I think that is adorable." Cathy remarked. "Come, let's go and sit down. I'll get us something cold to drink."

"Only two small bags?" Bill asked, looking at the sparse luggage.

"We plan to do some shopping while we are here. This is not purely a business trip—at least not anymore. Dottie has convinced me to start trusting others more, and that includes the company's daily operations. I'll explain later. Right now, I am parched."

"Clarissa and I can take the bags upstairs. I have two rooms ready for you." Doug said, picking up a piece of luggage.

"One room will suffice, right honey?" Dottie suggested.

Bob smiled. "One room will be fine and thank you."

Gaea and Vicky were in awe of Bob and Dorothy and chatted constantly during dinner. Both were fascinated by how things were printed, especially books. Bob indulged the girls with answers to their many questions in between pulling pieces of lobster from its shell, dipping the succulent meat into warm drawn butter, and eating it.

Jack and Jeremy were happily making a mess like the other six adults and two children, breaking open shells and giggling like a couple of kids. Cathy was enjoying every minute of it. She wasn't sure if the Shaw Manor dining room had ever seen so many adults around the table in its historic existence. The exception is birthday parties. She made a mental note that Vicky's tenth birthday was coming up soon, and it would be the first in her new home.

"Are you ready for your first book signing, Jack?" Bill asked. "It's just around the corner."

"Not really. I hate crowds of people. Too much chaos." He answered succinctly, feeling much more comfortable with Pender than he had thought he would. It didn't hurt that Jeremy was also sitting right next to him.

Bob tossed his napkin onto his plate. "Necessary, my dear boy, for your success. Without a fan base, you have nothing."

"I know. Bill has been telling me what to expect, and I can do it." Jack replied confidently, or at least he hoped it sounded confident.

"Smile, sign, and move on to the next. It goes quick." The author added. "It's the damn appearances that I have to speak at that are truly horrific."

"Bill." Cathy scolded.

"Sorry, I meant darn."

"These are simple signings," Pepper said. "I had planned on overseeing all of them…"

Bill groaned.

"But circumstances have changed and, if I may, changed for the better. I've canceled all but two of the signings. You both will be doing a single day at the Portland Civic Center and another at the Metropolitan Literature Convention Hall in Boston. I will be at the one in Portland for a brief time. I'm interested to see a book signing as I've never been to one."

Bill stared at his publisher, his mouth agape. "How…"

"My lovely wife-to-be and secretary extraordinaire, of course. She is a magician when it comes to things such as these. And I have been informed to leave this to the professionals. Clarissa is a pro, and with the help of Jeremy as well as the rest of the production crew, I can leave it to them and take a trip up the coast of Maine. I'm excited to visit Bar Harbor and Mount Desert Island with Dottie."

Bill stood up, walked around the table, and knelt before Dorothy. "My lady, most beautiful and gracious. Thank you for saving me."

Everyone laughed except for the girls. "Weirdo," Gaea whispered into her friend's ear.

Jeremy, Jack, and the girls were lying in front of the fireplace, watching another movie and sharing a large bowl of popcorn. Piddles had chosen Jack's lap to lie on. Everyone else sat at the kitchen table enjoying after-dinner drinks. Not one of them was drinking alcohol, to the astonishment of Bill, who himself had opened a bottle of lemonade. The two-hundred-and-fifty-dollar bottle of scotch he had bought sat unopened in the cabinet of the bar. Instead, Bob Pepper had chosen Diet Dew. Cathy rarely drank, Clarissa opted for sparkling water, and Doug happily sipped on a tall glass of iced tea. Dottie had an untouched glass of ice water sitting in front of her.

They all talked well into the evening long after the movie had ended, and Gaea and Vicky had headed off to bed.

CHAPTER 22
The Statue

"Shaw Manor seems so empty," Cathy said, taking a sip of her coffee.

Doug put a small amount of stevia into his coffee and stirred it. "And thankfully quiet as well."

"What time is the medium supposed to arrive?"

"Clarissa said before noon, but I guess that depends if his flight is on time and the traffic coming out of Logan."

She nodded and reached for the carton of cream. "I just can't believe it is happening again after all these years. Bill and I did right by the house and the Shaws and kept the manor as close to how the captain had it built."

"Look, I'm no ghost hunter, but I do believe in the paranormal." He looked at Cathy and continued. "I spent my childhood living in a haunted house. My mother, sister, and I were terrorized constantly by black shadows, apparitions, and sounds that would make one's blood curdle. It went on for almost six years."

"Why not move? Why did she put up will it?"

"Move where? Mom became a widow when my dad was involved in a car accident. She didn't have many skills as she chose to forego college and become a stay-at-home mother. When Dad died, it nearly broke her will. Everything she had was invested in the house. If it wasn't for me and my sister, I'm not sure she would have lived for as long as she did. Putting us first, she started working two jobs: a waitress at a local café and a nurse's aide at a nursing home. When the haunting began, Karen, my older sister, had to step up and look after me. She was fifteen at the time. When she graduated, she moved out and it was just me and mom."

"That's horrible."

Doug shrugged. "I can't blame Karen for leaving. I would have done the same if I could."

"What happened?"

"Mom died of breast cancer when I was seventeen; I was sent to live with a relative and his wife. It was all well and good. Because of them, I was able to go to college and get my degree."

"And the house?"

"Karen sold it and with the profit we shared, it helped me to pursue my doctorate. I never returned to that damned place. Why would I want to?"

Cathy stood up and refilled her cup. "More?"

He waved her off. "One is more than enough. I keep forgetting to buy some decaf when I'm out. This jet fuel gives me the jitters, and it's not good for the ticker." He said, laughing.

"I wish you and Clarissa lived closer. We don't have friends here in town. Having a husband who is a celebrity has its drawbacks. We have Gaea's friends and their parents over from time to time, and as you know, I lost my best friend."

"Tracy. Of course, I do."

She nodded and leaned against the bar. "I miss her."

"Are you nervous about today?" He asked, steering the subject away from her dead friend.

"A little. I've never had a psychic medium in my home before. I don't know what to expect."

"In my experience, expect the unexpected." Doug noticed Cathy's apprehension. "Look, Kirk Dirkins is world-renowned in the paranormal field. I met the man once a few years ago, and his professionalism is only outdone by his results. I'm going to be right here with you when he tells us what he finds."

Cathy reached into her apron pocket and placed a ring of keys on the table. "To unlock the attic door as well as the basement. He needs full access to all areas of the house, right?"

"Yes," Doug said, picking them up.

Bill was enjoying himself as he signed book after book. Sitting next to him, Jack was also busy dealing with his own fans, which had grown exponentially in numbers in the short time since his book release… Bill could take breaks and when he did, Jack continued, and people didn't seem to mind the interruptions. Bob Pepper had come and gone without so much as a hello or goodbye.

Bill was also surprised when a fan presented him with a tee shirt to sign. He had looked at Clarissa, and she smiled. During a break, she told him that it was Bob's idea to sell shirts as a promotion for his newly published best-seller, and she had readily agreed. Bill had to admit that they were nice as the book cover art had been printed on them. Four colors and assorted sizes seemed to be flying off the shelves. The cut from the sales made the author happier as well. He figured not signing the merchandise contract prior to the release was a small detail. His agent did have liberties when it came to the Bill Pender brand.

Jeremy and a young female crew member had taken the girls to explore and shop in Portland. He was a little nervous that his two daughters might just buy everything in the city. For some reason, he trusted Jack's boyfriend and hoped all would be fine.

Bill was more concerned about Cathy and Doug and their meeting with the psychic medium. It was the second time that business had prevented him from being present during a serious matter such as this. He had all the confidence in his wife's ability to manage any situation; however, Doug being there with her gave him comfort.

Over the years, Bill had come to consider him a close friend. Being a famed writer didn't help his situation when it came to male friends. The location of the estate was a hindrance as well. The size of the property secluded the manor on the part of Cape Neddick where it was built. The houses that were nearby were primarily seasonal homes, and a lot of them were rentals. During the winter, the neighborhood became somewhat of a ghost town. He had made friends with an elderly man shortly after the renovation. However, the gentleman passed away the following winter. His house had been sold, and now it was another rental.

Clarissa walked up to him and handed him a shirt. "Time to go back to work."

Bill took it and looked at his agent. "I am not a rock star, and you are a bitch." He said, smiling.

"But you are a darling, and yes, I am one. Now, put the damn thing on."

The doorbell of the Shaw Manor rang precisely at five past noon, and when Cathy opened the door, she was greeted by a middle-aged man wearing dark sunglasses and a younger woman, her arm clasped to his at the crook of the elbow. He was dressed in denim jeans, a simple gray polo shirt, and white tennis shoes. His wiry hair was stark white, and he brushed his shoulders. She, in contrast, wore a bright blue flowered short dress, black combat boots, and her jet-black hair accented her intense blue eyes.

"Hello," the man said, holding out his hand. I am Professor Dirkins, and this is my lovely daughter Jackie. We are here to assist you if we can."

Cathy at once realized that the man was blind as she took his hand. "Thank you for taking the time to come. We seem to have a problem."

"Professor Dirkins!" Doug exclaimed, approaching the guests.

"I know that voice. That would be Dr. Douglas Drake, the esteemed psychologist. How are you, young man?"

"Great, and far from young." He replied, grasping the older man's hand. "Come in."

The two stepped into the foyer, and Dirkins placed his hand on a settee. "Can I sit here? I like to take time to talk and get a feel for the place I am in."

"Of course," Cathy said. "Please sit down."

Moments later, Dirkins spoke. "I can feel the water upon the rocks. It reverberates through the house. This is a large house?"

"Very large," Cathy answered. "It's a manor."

"I can feel something...something from above. And this house is built on solid rock."

"It is." Doug added. "There is a very small space below that houses the boiler."

Dirkins waved the comment off. "That is of no consequence here. I want to go upstairs. There is something..." He paused, looking up with blind eyes. "Something, but maybe nothing. How do I get there?" He said, standing up.

"Right over here professor," Cathy said. "The grand staircase is the most direct way."

"Take me, Jackie. Catherine, if you and Douglas will remain down here, my daughter and I will proceed."

"Of course," Cathy said.

"Professor," Doug said, handing Jackie the key ring. I'm handing your daughter the key that will unlock the attic door. It has been locked since the incident."

The professor nodded as his daughter led him to the stairs. He grasped the handrail and said, "Lovely manor."

"What does the ocean and the rock have to do with this?" Cathy asked. The two had retreated to the far side of the great room and sat together on the sofa.

"It is believed by experts that moving water is attributed to the energy that a spirit needs to manifest. A stream that passes underneath a building, for example. As for the rock, it is believed that certain types, such as limestone quartz, can retain memories of an event and will release the trapped movie, for lack of a better word, from time to time."

"Replaying the event that occurred near to the rock?"

"Right. The rock we are sitting on, I am guessing it is dark gabbro, which is common here on Cape Neddick."

"Dark gabbro?"

He laughed. "Otherwise known as black granite."

"Ah. I didn't know you were a geologist." Cathy teased.

"Me? Internet research. I thought it would be a good idea to look up a few things."

"Very wise, Doug." She said, reaching down to pet the dog. "I think she misses Gaea and Vicky."

Jackie led her father down the long hallway and back toward the grand staircase. From the dozens of cases she had accompanied him on, she knew not to offer suggestions and to remain silent except for the odd comment concerning safety, such as a stairway. He stopped directly in front of the padlocked door. "You have the key. Please unlock and open the door."

The girl did as she was told, and after removing the two locks, the newly hung door swung quietly open.

"What do you see?" Her father asked her the familiar starting question.

"There are narrow wooden stairs leading up into a very dimly lit space. I think there is a light at the top."

"What does a blind man have need of an electric light?"

"Well, for me…"

"You will remain here," Dirkins instructed his daughter.

"But Dad."

He touched his daughter lightly with his hand. "There is no danger up there. I feel fear and sadness but nothing threatening. Now, is there something to hold onto?"

"Of course." She said, and she guided him to the handrail.

"I won't be long."

"OK."

"Another couple of hours and we are going to shut it down, Bill," Clarissa informed her star author. "All of the shirts and books have been sold for you and Jack. It looks like only a couple hundred or so people are left in line."

"That's it? The fantastic writer extraordinaire Bill Pender only has two hundred fans left to greet. I'm appalled." He said, grinning.

She leaned forward and whispered in his ear. "I think they are here for Jack."

At the bottom of the stairwell Jackie could hear her father but was not able to make out what he was saying. A conversation of sorts, but it was all muffled. It seemed to her that he was talking to himself, and she hated it. As the minutes passed, being left out of a part of an investigation made her blood boil. Partly because she was not there to help him, but mostly because she, as a paranormal investigator was being brushed aside, and it was infuriating. She understood his fatherly desire to protect her, but it became unbearable at times such as this. It took everything within her not to charge up the stairs, and she had come close to doing just that when he appeared and began to walk down.

The professor hugged his daughter and reassured her that all was well. "We need to go across the hall. I want you to go with me. Open the door, please." As they entered the master bedroom she waited as her father gathered his thoughts and impressions.

"There is a separate space above, not part of the attic." He began. "Is there a way up in this room?"

"The room is large, and there is a spiral staircase to your left on the opposite side of the bed that leads up."

"Lead me up, Jackie."

"That is not a squall." Captain Lars Enstrom of the Archaean Horizon said quietly to his first officer. "It looks like a building tropical storm."

"That's not possible, captain." She stated. "This far north?"

"It's not unheard of. Craig, are we still sending data to NOAA?" He asked his technician.

"Yes, sir, all systems transmit normally to all monitoring services except one. Weather Canada Nova Scotia seems to be down. I will try to reestablish the link."

The captain nodded and walked to the bank of weather monitoring equipment that the ship had. "Doppler seems to be off the charts. Look at it. It's wrapping, and if I am not mistaken, it looks like a spin is starting to form. And the ship's barometer is dropping. Something is not right." He walked to the front of the bridge and held his binoculars up to his eyes.

"Anything, captain?" Patricia Hilton asked. The young woman had been hired on as first officer and had proven to be more than capable of performing her duties. The captain considered her as a candidate to replace him once he retired upon completing this voyage.

"No, but my gut is telling me otherwise. I've learned over my many years at sea to expect anything and count on nothing. The sea can be a cruel creature."

"Aye, sir."

The Swedish captain turned and scratched his chin. "What would you advise, Patricia?"

"Monitor the situation and make sure our readings are correct and being transmitted to the proper weather centers as per protocol. Contact the Coast Guard and inform them of our present position and that we are not currently in danger and are able to give aid if needed."

"And our own ship and crew?"

She looked back at the monitors for a moment. "I would order the decks secured and prepared for inclement weather."

"Batten down the hatches?" The captain inquired.

She answered without hesitation. "Yes. The ship needs to be prepared for its safety as well as the crew."

"Anything else?" Enstrom prompted.

"Contact a safe port and make way as soon as possible."

"Any place in mind?"

"Portland. Sir. It is the closest harbor that can take a ship of this tonnage. Sir."

The old captain smiled and nodded. "Carry it out, first officer. Prepare the Archaean Horizon, contact the harbor master at Portland and prepare to make way. I will go below and speak to our doctors.

Take the helm, Patricia. And have the boatswain double-check the lifeboats just to be sure. We will make the best speed once ready."

"Aye, captain."

"It's a library, Dad," Jackie said to Professor Dirkins, admiring the widow's watch. "It's round with books encircling half the room. There are two French doors that face the ocean and a small balcony a person could step out on. There is a desk as well in the center of the room facing the sea. Quite lovely."

The professor stood stoically for a moment, then felt his way to the beginning of the bookshelves. "Bill Pender's office. What did he call it? His dreamer's hideaway?"

"His wife said that is what his daughter calls it."

"There is something not right here. A presence, an incredibly old presence that I can't quite place. Is there anything in the room that looks out of sorts? Something that doesn't seem to belong?"

"Nothing I wouldn't expect to see in a library," Jackie answered.

"Tell me what you see, " her father said, continuing to examine the shelves with his hands.

"Lots of books and some knickknacks placed here and there. Nothing special. Nautical stuff such as a miniature lobster trap, a barometer, and seagull figurines. The only thing on the desk is a computer and an old-fashioned quill lying next to a pot of ink. Other than a family picture, the desk is neat and clean."

"There was something here." He said, touching the void that once held the Constance deck logs. "No. No bother. It is of no consequence. What else is in the room?"

"Two fake potted plants, what appears to be an antique rug that I am guessing to be a Bokhara and an Egyptian statue that stands about three feet tall."

"Describe the statue, please."

"As I said, about three feet tall, and it's black with gold inlay on the clothing. It appears to be an animal; I think a dog."

"Take me to it." She led her father to the far side of the room and guided his hand to the head of the statue. His fingers glided carefully over the smooth surface. "Alabaster, but not right. You say it looks like a dog?"

"Yes."

"Curious." He said, continuing to run his hand over the head of the statue, feeling its ears. "Too short. This cannot be a true Anubis statue. Still, there is something."

"Anubis?"

"Yes, the Egyptian god of the underworld. And not a dog but a man with the head of a jackal. It was quite revered when it came to the ancients and their beliefs in the afterlife. Anubis was a guardian. Priests would dress as the god as they performed the mummification rituals, blessing the corpse with prayers and oils to ensure that Anubis would guide them through the afterworld, where they were to be judged by the god Osiris, who would grant them eternal life. Fascinating."

"Father!" Jackie exclaimed, pulling him away from the statue. "It's eyes! They are glowing red!"

He fell back, shaking violently. "Powerful and evil, " he said weakly. Let us leave this place."

CHAPTER 23
Bar Harbor & Escalations

Bill was quite happy as the entire book signing affair had wrapped up on schedule. Having Jack along had proven to be a blessing for his normally frayed nerves that came to the surface on such occasions. He made a mental note to recommend to Bob Pepper that book signings be conducted with more than one author. The extra crew, as well as having an agent such as Clarissa to organize the circus, was a boon. He was able to take breaks and not have to chase down lunch as it was delivered by staff in the green room. Bill had been able to call Cathy a couple of times, and as he leaned against a wall away from the dispersing crowd, he reached for his phone and called home.

"Hello," Cathy answered after a single ring. "Where are you?"

He could hear that she had been crying, and something was not right. "Babe, what is going on? We're leaving for home shortly. Just waiting on the limo."

Cathy sobbed into the phone as she tried to talk. "I think the psychic medium had a heart attack, and the paramedics are here. He keeps mumbling, "It's evil", and his daughter is freaking out."

"Cathy, what's evil? I don't understand."

"Please…"

The line went silent. He tried frantically to return his wife's call only to receive a busy signal. On the fourth attempt, his own cell phone went dead. "Dammit, Bill. Charge the damn thing, you idiot." He stuffed it into his back pocket and looked around. "Clarissa! I am leaving, limo or not." He yelled.

She appeared from the staging area. "Bill, what, for Christ's sake, is wrong?"

"Problems at home. Either you get that car here now or I am grabbing a cab. Where are the girls?"

"It's here. Gaea, Vicky, Jack, and Jeremy are already in it. We are waiting for you. Why are you back here in the green room?"

He rolled his eyes. "I was trying to call Cathy, then the damn phone died. Did my daughters have a fun time?" He asked, attempting to switch gears inside his own mind and focus on the now.

"Splendid. Lots of bags from shopping."

"I need to get back to the manor."

"Let's go. Tell me on the way, okay? You can call Cathy with my phone." Clarissa said as she handed him her cell phone.

"Fine." Bill followed her out into the alley, and they climbed into the limousine. Jack and Jeremy were curled up together, sound asleep. The girls were also curled up in the seats opposite the guys and were playing a video game. "Hi, Dad." The two said and returned to their game. Clarissa shrugged as they sped off toward Cape Neddick.

"Bobby, it's beautiful," Dorothy said, examining the diamond ring on her finger.

"It's a tad small. Don't you think?" He said with a big grin.

"It's perfect. You know I don't like gaudy things. I rarely wear jewelry, but I do love this. And the wedding bands we picked are lovely."

He smiled and took her hand. "Tradition dictates that we are supposed to buy each other's band. Screw tradition. I loved shopping for them with you, Dottie, and I think we made a great choice."

"Me too. I've always preferred sterling over gold." She affirmed.

The limousine driver opened the rear cab window and called back, "Mr. Pepper, we are going to be at your first destination shortly."

"Thank you."

"What are you up to?" She asked.

"Town Hall of Bar Harbor. We can't get married without a license now, can we?"

She became wide-eyed. "You sly old fox!"

"Let's get married in Maine, Dorothy. There is no sense in waiting, is there?"

"Robert Pepper, I would love to marry you in this beautiful place. It is so magical."

"I'm glad you agree because the fun is just starting."

It took less than an hour for the couple to obtain their license to marry. Early that afternoon, they were onboarding a sailboat heading out through the Mount Desert Narrows and into the Gulf of Maine. The North Atlantic Ocean was calm except for an occasional wave that broke against the Seal Queen's bow, sending cold salty spray into the air and over the couple. The captain of the boat held a Bible in his hands and delivered the Rites of Marriage as the first mate kept the boat on course. As the schooner cut through the narrows at full sail, Dottie was awestruck by the beauty of nature that presented itself. Seagulls screeched and soared, circling the stern of the boat, hoping for a morsel to be tossed. Seals barked on the shoreline that made up Acadia National Park and frolicked in the frigid water, grasping fish before climbing back upon the jagged rocks, a backdrop of evergreen trees towering into the air. "Beautiful." She whispered. Two hours later, they were wed.

"You may kiss her now." The captain said, closing the book. "Ayuh, you are married, and it's legal. I'm a captain and the minister of my church. I would like for ya to come by Sunday mornin' if so inclined. The sermon starts at ten in the mornin' sharp. Sunday school at nine if you have young ones."

Bob pulled his bride to him and kissed her. "It seems that people on the island have multiple duties," Bob said.

"I think it is wonderful." She replied.

"Smitty, turn her 'round. Time to head home. But let us sail 'round the Cranberry's first."

"Aye."

"Keep an eye." The captain said to the couple. "Whales may breach, especially around the Cranberry Islands. Quite a sight if I might say so, especially if there is a Humpback about. Might even see a White. Big sharks up here from time to time. They like the seal pups."

Dottie grasped her husband's hand as the boat turned into the wind.

"Another freak storm?" Dr. Tarpon asked as he set the magnifying glass and brush down and rubbed his forehead. He could feel the onset of a headache. "What is it?"

The captain of the Archaean Horizon took a sip of his coffee. "We have aspirin in the ship's sick bay. Doctor, it's nothing to concern ourselves with. It appears to be sub-tropical with a chance to intensify. I expect it should only stir things up a bit."

"Lars, it is the stir-up that I am concerned with. We haven't finished the archeological examination of Constance. Another storm and we could lose valuable artifacts, not to mention the data."

"Jeffrey, I have sailed as the Archaean Horizon's captain for as long as you have owned her. I have been through hell and back with you, guiding her through the seven seas and beyond. Safety of the crew first. Don't you trust me?"

"Of course, I do old salt. It's just frustrating. So, what is my captain's plan?"

"Secure the ship and head for Portland Harbor. Lay up until the storm passes. I have my first preparing as we speak."

"She is a good officer, isn't she?" Jeff asked.

"Very capable young woman. She will make a fine captain."

"You are recommending her for captaincy of the Horizon?"

"I am."

The doctor sighed and placed his hand on the man's shoulder. "You are still set on retiring."

"Aye. Not from the sea, just from the responsibility. I'm getting old and I think I still have a few years left of doing some fishing down in the Florida Keys. Just me and a small flat boat."

"You have been a good friend Lars. And a damn fine skipper for my ship and her crew. I'm going to miss you dearly."

The old man smiled weakly. "I best be notifying the crew of our return to port and checking on the bridge."

Releasing his captain from a brief hug, Tarpon returned to examining a rusted pocket watch.

The limousine screeched to a halt in front of Shaw Manor, and Gaea and Vicky jumped out, running toward Cathy. She stood on the porch and looked visibly upset. There was no sign of police or an ambulance, which gave Bill relief. There was also no sign of Doug. Cathy hugged her girls and shooed them into the house to an excited Piddles. Standing up, she placed her hands on her hips. She was angry.

Bill was nervous. He had been able to call his wife using his agent's phone, but the information that Cathy had conveyed was sketchy at best. A heart attack, a death, and a girl who was in hysterics. Something about evil being spoken had shaken him. The signal had broken up numerous times due to a few cell tower failures in southern

Maine, and the weather wasn't helping the situation. A storm was rapidly approaching the coast. Light rain was already falling as Jeremy and Jack exited the car and ran for the manor. Something was terribly wrong, and he could feel it.

Jeremy and Jack took the girls upstairs as the other adults gathered in a closed dining room talking quietly.

"Bill, it's starting again," Cathy said. "Something is not right in our home."

"Cathy," Doug began, "we were all here for that, well, thing back then. How can we be sure it is the same?"

"We can't," Clarissa said flatly. "Things have changed."

"She is right," Bill said, taking a sip of scotch and wincing at the taste. Cathy looked at him and frowned. "Sorry, babe. Just a nerve calmer."

"Pour the shit out."

He placed the glass on the table and pushed it away. "OK. Let's look at the facts. What has changed? The manor has been peaceful for a decade. We did go through hell. All of us did. So, what is the difference now?"

"Victoria," Cathy admitted.

"Honey, I find it hard to believe that a ten-year-old girl is causing this."

"Bill, that man had a heart attack in your office and kept mumbling 'evil' and 'get rid of it'. I thought he was going to die on our floor."

"I find that a psychic having a heart attack and mumbling incoherently scientific proof of nothing," Doug added.

"Neither is a house that was held together in pristine condition for decades by a ghost scientifically feasible." Bill countered. "But Shaw Manor was. We lived through it, Doug."

"And my best friend died here. In the same room where this man nearly did."

"Technically, Tracy didn't die in the widow's watch."

"Oh, come off it, Bill. Something caused her to jump from the balcony. And I do not think for a moment it was some lame psychiatrist's postmortem diagnosis of depression leading to suicide. I met my best friend, and she was a very happy girl. No offense, Doug."

"None taken." He stood up and reached for the glass of scotch. "Do you mind, Bill?"

Bill shook his head and held his hands up in surrender toward his wife. "I'm sorry, babe."

"The study of the mind is my profession, but I am no parapsychologist and don't pretend to be. That being said, there must be something that is causing this haunting. What is different? I also do not buy that Vicky is the problem. Perhaps a combination of things." He walked to the window, pushed the curtain aside, and looked out over the manor's courtyard. "What are we overlooking?" Doug was interrupted by a loud crash and screaming from above.

"Now what?" Bill said, charging toward the door, followed by Doug, Clarissa, and Cathy. "I'm getting sick of this."

Jack and Jeremy had seen to the girls and sat with them in their bedroom. The four ate from a bag of saltwater taffy that Jeremy had bought while the girls had shopped around the boutiques that dotted the Old Port.

"I don't like the licorice ones," Jack said.

"I do. Give it to me!" Vicky exclaimed.

He handed it to her and reached for a strawberry. "These are much better, right Jer?"

Jeremy smiled, unwrapping a blackberry. "He never did like them, even when we were your age, " he said before biting down and pulling the candy out from his face. The girls laughed and tried to mimic him, stretching the candy until it snapped, breaking back onto their faces.

"You two have been friends for a long time," Gaea commented.

"Since before I can remember. We grew up together. Jack has been my best friend, and there is nothing I wouldn't do for him."

"Ditto, Jer."

"Kind of like Vicky and me," Gaea said, smiling.

"I'm thirsty."

"Me too, Vicky. I'll run downstairs and get us some bottled water." Jeremy said, climbing off the bed. "Saltwater taffy will do that to ya." He walked out, heading for the grand staircase, when the master bedroom door exploded outward, sending Jeremy tumbling down to the first landing, his head hitting the wall, knocking him unconscious. Shattered and splintered wood fell around and on top of his limp body. Jack ran from the room and picked his way through debris, trying to get to Jeremy. The girls huddled together at the head of the bed and screamed.

The limousine carrying the newlyweds headed southeast from Bar Harbor, heading to what Bob Pepper hoped would be a new chapter in his life. He had become tired of New York City and the daily grind of keeping his family's business relevant in the competitive world of publishing. As he had done most of his life, Robert F Pepper made a wager betting on his future. The initial stake had paid off, and she was now sitting next to him. The second was the hire of a young general manager who would take control of day-to-day operations. Thirty-two-year-old Liz Aquaro didn't have a ton of experience, but the Puerto Rican had graduated from the NYC School of Business and Law at the top of her class. During their three-hour interview, he had been impressed with her fiery passion and desire to succeed. Bob had intentionally sent Dorothy off on some random company errand to keep his plans secretive.

Bob smiled as he looked out the window at the mountains in the distance. The new home he had purchased rivaled that of Bill Pender's. The old mansion sat on Sols Cliff Road overlooking the North Atlantic Ocean and towering upon a ledge that dropped far below to waves that never ceased crashing upon jagged rocks, sending water high enough into the air that the spray nearly reached the edge of the property.

He had never set foot in the place and relied solely on telephone calls, pictures, and correspondence from the realtor. Seventeen bedrooms and ten and a half baths would be more than enough for himself and Dottie and any guests that might be invited to visit. The eight acres of land and the remoteness had finally sealed the deal for him. Not that he felt the need for privacy, but his clients did. One thing that Bob had come to realize over his years as the CEO of Pepper & Pepper was that nearly all his authors held their own privacy close. The new mansion would be an ideal getaway on certain occasions when needed. He sold his penthouse condo in Manhattan along with most of its contents to be able to finance the new house. He had a small truckload of personal items sent up to his new home long before he and Dottie had left for Maine. Win or fail, Bob Pepper was fully committed to spending the rest of his life in Maine.

Keeping his role as the owner of the company would not change as he wasn't ready to sell the publishing house. There was still too much of himself and too many years invested. Stepping away from some of the highly stressful decisions was a good compromise. He also had his health to consider, although that had become less of an issue with some hard and serious life changes. Giving up the booze, cigars, and fat-filled foods for a beautiful wife was the best decision he had ever made, both for business and his personal life. The limo pulled up to the stately mansion, and Dorothy squeezed his hand.

"You didn't tell me we are going to honeymoon at a lovely inn on the island."

Bob smiled and reached into his lapel pocket. He placed a key into the palm of her hand and said, "Welcome home."

Bill leaped up to the first landing. "Doug, check on Jeremy."

"Got it. Go check on the girls."

He looked caringly at Jack before climbing up to the hallway. Cathy and Clarissa stopped at the base of the stairs, and Doug looked back at them. "It's too dangerous. Go around." Clarissa turned and ran toward the back stairs. Cathy ignored the warning and climbed up and through the debris.

Bill found his daughters huddled together and sobbing hysterically. He hugged them both tightly and rocked them gently. "What happened?" Both girls shook their heads. A moment later, Cathy entered the room, jumped onto the bed, and joined her family. "They are okay." He assured her. "I'm going to go see what the hell happened." Cathy nodded as he ran back into the hall meeting a very frightened Clarissa. "Cathy is with the girls; they are okay," Bill informed her. She nodded and went into the bedroom to join them.

Bill walked through what was left of the master bedroom doorway. The door had been completely ripped away from its jamb and looked partially destroyed. What he walked into stunned him. Not a thing was out of place. The bed was perfectly made. Paintings and pictures hung from the walls in their appropriate places. The curtains hung as they always did, and not so much as a knickknack was out of place.

He walked to the bathroom and opened the door. Again, nothing was amiss. Opening the walk-in closet door, Bill reached in and flipped the switch. The light that filled the space showed that no shoe had been disturbed.

"What the hell?" He muttered.

Bill turned his attention to the wrought iron spiral staircase that led to the widow's watch. Grasping the handrail, he began to slowly climb upward, turning his head to try to see above. The sun had left the eastern sky and had passed over the manor casting the widow's watch into shadows, passing into night. His heart pounded in his chest as he grasped the cold iron and forced himself to climb further up until he could see the legs of his desk and chair. The French doors were closed, and the room was eerily quiet.

"Bill!"

He spun around and nearly fell. "What the hell, Cathy? You scared the hell out of me!" She flipped a switch at the bottom of the stairs. "Turn the light on before you kill yourself."

"Everything is fine. As fine as can be expected. What is going on?" He said, using his shirt to wipe the sweat from his face. "Is everyone OK?"

"They are downstairs in the great room. Clarissa has the girls calmed down, although they are very frightened. Thankfully, Jeremy only has a bump on his head, and Jack attends to him. Doug removed the largest parts of what was left of our bedroom door, partially clearing the stairs. Come down, we need to talk."

Bill nodded and collected himself. As he took the first step to go down, he heard a low growl coming from the library above.

CHAPTER 24
Decisions & Dirkins

Clarissa walked into the manor and hung up her phone, slumping onto the sofa. "Well, believe it or not, he agrees, and you are not going to believe this, Bill."

"Believe what?" Bill said, pouring himself a glass of iced tea followed by a healthy shot of vodka. He sat down next to his wife. "Sorry, babe, but today was hell." She took the glass from his hand and nearly drained it.

"Well, I guess a refill then?" She asked, holding the glass up. Doug took the glass from Cathy and went to the bar. "Let me." He offered.

Clarissa crossed her legs and arms and looked at Bill. "First of all, our publisher is married."

"What?"

"The old bastard up and eloped with his secretary and that is not all. He sold his condo in New York, hired a general manager for the company, and bought a mansion up in Bar Harbor. He and Dorothy are up there right now." She told them. Bill was able to muster a chuckle.

"What is so funny, Bill?" Cathy said sternly.

"I'm sorry, it's just that I can never put anything past Bob Pepper. It's the only piece of good news I have heard throughout this miserable piece of shit day."

Doug handed Cathy and Bill their glasses. "Clair, you want a drink?"

"No, there is more," Clarissa answered. "No alcohol for me."

"Okay." He said and went to pour himself a scotch.

"So, what else?" Cathy asked, taking a sip of her drink.

"I spent the better part of an hour talking to Bob. I explained in not too much detail what is going on here."

Bill nodded. "He knows of what happened before, although I'm not sure he believes it."

"Believing is not necessarily caring. He wants Cathy and me to bring the girls up to Mount Desert Island while you and Doug straighten this mess out."

"I am not going," Cathy said flatly.

"Honey." Bill implored.

"I was here for the first haunting, and I am damn certain I am not running away from this. Clarissa, will you please…"

"Of course." She interrupted. "I understand."

The girls had been sitting quietly with Jeremy and Jack when Gaea spoke up. "Mom, I don't want to be sent away."

"Me neither," Vicky said.

"It's not what's in the attic." Gaea began. "I know that now. Rebecca and Tracy are nice ghosts. They come and see me sometimes." Cathy dropped her drink onto the floor.

Vicky became angry. "Gaea! Rebecca scratched me!"

She smiled at her friend and pulled her in for a hug. "That was not Rebecca, my darling."

"Gaea, what are you talking about?" Her father asked. "What do you know about Tracy?"

"I know what she tells me."

"And what does she tell you?" Clarissa asked, moving to the edge of the sofa, intent on hearing what the child was saying.

"Well, she says she was here for a party to be with her friends. I think it was for you, Mom. She said she was with a bunch of other girls looking at the house when she was left behind upstairs. She was looking at the water when she was scared by something and fell over the balcony." Gaea explained. Cathy began to tear up. "She didn't jump, mommy," Gaea said knowingly. Cathy fell against her husband, and he stroked her hair.

"I knew it." Cathy sobbed, and her phone rang.

"Let me take it, babe." Bill took her phone and looked at the screen. "It's the psychic medium, I think. That Dirkins guy." Cathy grabbed her phone from his hand, stood up, and ran into the kitchen.

"Gaea, look at this scratch," Vicky said, pointing to her arm. Gaea looked at the girl's arm and raised her eyebrows. "Well, it was there," Vicky said defensively.

"I know, but it wasn't Rebecca. Trust me."

They all watched Cathy as she paced back and forth in the kitchen. She kept glancing up at the ceiling, which made Bill extremely nervous.

"We haven't even had time to settle in, Dottie," Bob said, taking laundry out of the washing machine and stuffing it into the dryer.

"We've had plenty of time, and I am overjoyed by what you have done for us, although a smaller house would have sufficed. How am I going to keep this monstrosity clean, let alone take care of my secretarial duties?" Dottie asked.

Bob smiled. "We have gone through this. No more secretarial duties, or at least not as they used to be. The city life is over. All company business is going to be done from right here in this house."

"What if there is an emergency back at the publishing house? A coffee shortage or something?"

"I hardly think a shortage of coffee to be a company emergency, but we still have the corporate jet, and the Bangor airport is not far away. I don't plan to take any trips back to New York unless necessary. This new video conferencing thing I had installed upstairs should do fine for any meetings I have to attend. Honey, I am officially semi-retired."

"Semi is the problem with that statement. And computers. I don't trust the lot of them. An old-fashioned Royal typewriter did fine for me."

He laughed loudly. "I still have that old typewriter somewhere. Dottie, do you want me here or back in the city?"

"Here, of course." She smiled and looked up at her husband. "Now, we have children and guests coming, and I need to make up the rooms. You, Robert Pepper, keep doing this laundry. The sheets and towels smell musty, and we still need to wash everything in the kitchen. I will not serve meals on dusty dishware."

After the last load went into the dryer, he was able to go to his office on the third floor of the mansion. His beloved desk had been delivered prior to him and Dorothy moving in. Some items he decided to leave for the discretion of his new general manager. If she didn't want the sofa, wet bar, and other things, then so be it. Most of it reeked of years of cigar smoke. Along with the desk, he kept his leather chair, an antique Tiffany table lamp, and one piece of art he had sent to be professionally cleaned. The century-old oil painting was of a landscape he later discovered through a curator of the Maine coastline near Penobscot, another weekend getaway he would take with Dottie.

The new "smart TV" was large and took up most of the south wall of the office. The only things on his desk now were the lamp, a wireless keyboard, a mouse sitting on a Pepper & Pepper company pad, and a remote control. Simple telephone calls were now contained in his cell phone. There was no need for his old office telephone with dozens of extension buttons to call the various people within the company he used to talk to daily.

Robert picked up the remote control and pushed the power button. A chime sounded from the TV, and it produced a menu. Live TV, recorded choices, favorites, pay-per-view, and conferencing were just a few of them. Bob chose conferencing, and a submenu appeared. He chose video call and then Liz Aquaro's name. A metallic ringing followed as the screen showed a rotating circle. Moments later, the call request ended with a message that read, "The party is not answering. Would you like to try again?" He pressed the power button shutting the monitor off.

Standing up, Bob walked to the large bank of windows and doors that dominated the entire east wall of the office. Opening one of them, he stepped out onto the terrace and into a brisk chilly wind. The smells of the ocean flooded his senses, and he could not help but breathe in deeply. Hundreds of seagulls flew below him, trying to find a morsel of food left from the seals that clamored on the rocks.

He looked out over the Atlantic and shook his head. Children are already coming to the Pepper mansion. Bob had never thought about marriage, let alone having children. The company had always come first, and now he was regretting the time lost. There were times during his life that women had come and gone romantically. Now, he wasn't sure he could remember most of their names. Money could buy many things, and sex was one of them. He had never had a need for the unbridled pleasures that many men in New York City pursued. He had been to places such as Studio 54, but they never caught his fancy. Bob was dedicated to his father's dream, and the publishing house became his passion, and it has remained so until now.

Another brisk cold gust of wind brought him to his senses as his wife called to him. "Bobby? Are you up there? Dishes, remember?" Robert F Pepper grinned and tapped his forehead. "You're a married man now." He thought to himself. "Coming!" He called back to Dottie.

"And?" Bill asked his wife as she returned to the sitting area of the great room. "What did he say?"

"We have a demon in the house." She said flatly.

"Rebecca is not a demon!" Gaea said, standing up, her hands clenched into fists by her side. Cathy shook her head and then bent forward, placing her head in her hands.

"Gaea, your mother didn't say she was," Bill said, rubbing the back of his wife's neck.

"It's not Rebecca or Tracy, although according to Professor Dirkins, both of them are here in this house with us." Cathy continued.

"I told you they were," Gaea said, sitting down. "And both of them are terrified of what else is here with them…with us."

"Really, Cathy? A demon?" Clarissa asked sarcastically. "Isn't that kind of fairy tale-*ish*?"

"He didn't exactly say a demon. He described it as an evil and powerful presence."

"Powerful for sure. Just look at the bedroom. There is no logical explanation for what happened to that door with nothing out of place in the room." Doug added. "And the attic door."

Clarissa's phone alarmed. She pulled it from its holster and looked at it. "Wow, severe storm warning. Seems we are under a tropical storm warning. Sub-tropical. It says here to expect heavy wind and rains within the next twenty-four hours. The warning is from Portsmouth, New Hampshire, all the way up to Portland."

"Great, that is all we need." Bill stood up and went to the kitchen. "I'm taking the last Sam Adams, " he said, plucking the bottle from the refrigerator.

"Mommy, what are we going to do?" Vicky asked, squeezing her doll against her chest. "I'm afraid."

"You, my darlings, are going with me to visit a wonderful place up Maine," Clarissa said, kneeling before the two girls.

"What is so special about it?"

"Well, we are going to see some seals and maybe even a whale. Uncle Bob and Aunt Dottie are waiting for us in Bar Harbor."

"Do we have to go?" Gaea pleaded.

"You are going." Her father said. "And soon. With that storm moving in, I would like to see you on the road tonight, Clarissa. It's only a three-and-a-half, maybe four-hour drive max. Straight up the turnpike, then two ninety-five when you hit Portland. Take Cathy's, Range Rover. Is that okay, babe?"

Cathy nodded and pulled Gaea to her. "Please, honey. I need you to look after Vicky. Just for a few days, alright?"

She nodded. "Just for a few days. Can Jeremy and Jack come?"

Bill looked at the two young men questioningly. "I think that would be a good idea. The Boston gig is officially on hold as of now. Jeremy, the girls like and trust you."

"The question is, do you trust me?" Jeremy asked.

"I do," Bill said confidently. "Jack, you in?"

"Whatever Jer says."

"Okay, we seem to have at least a basic plan of action. Clair, get the car out of the garage. Doug, go upstairs and pack a bag for the girls. You two go get your bags packed as well." Bill instructed.

"They are packed. After what happened, I stuffed everything into the suitcases. I just need to go up and get them."

"Good thinking, Jeremy. Go with Doug and get them."

Less than an hour later, Bill, Cathy, and Doug waved as the Range Rover headed off to Bar Harbor. Piddles was already curled up in her travel crate, snoring. Dark clouds were passing rapidly overhead, and the wind had started to increase. "Maybe you should have gone with your wife," Bill said, hugging his.

"She will be fine. The girls need her, and you need me here. We are going to beat this." Doug responded.

Cathy broke down sobbing. "Honey, it's going to be okay," Bill assured her. She shook her head and looked at her husband. "I think this is all my fault."

"Cathy, no. That's not true."

"I think it is, Doug. I started all of this."

"Babe, that's not possible."

She looked at him coldly, and the word she uttered made his blood turn to ice in his veins. "Anubis."

The captain of the Archaean Horizon was not happy as he made his way onto the bridge. "First, report, dammit," Lars commanded.

"I have ordered the starboard engine shut down. I believe we have a fouled prop. The cooling temperatures were climbing quickly, and I feared losing the engine altogether."

"The engine would have shut down automatically when the temperatures approached critical. But still, a good precautionary decision." The captain acknowledged. "Of all the luck." He walked around the bridge, scanning the various computer stations before fixating on the Doppler radar. "Speed?"

"Eight knots, sir." The helmsman called out.

"Damn. The storm is moving faster than we are."

"We could stop and put divers in the water to clear the obstruction, sir." Hilton offered.

"We don't know what the obstruction is. A net, a rope, or something else. The sea is building. I will not risk putting men into the water and risking their lives. Nor will I risk the Aquabot in these seas. No, we will make the best speed to Portland. Notify the Coast Guard of our situation and ask them to monitor and stand by."

"Aye, captain."

CHAPTER 25
Ghosts in the Guesthouse

Clarissa was south of Portland when the first bands of subtropical storm Delilah came ashore. The gusts of wind and heavy rain made it difficult to see the road as their path twisted and turned ahead. Jeremy sat next to her, trying to help her navigate and read road signs. Jack sat with the girls in the back seat, keeping them occupied with some sort of pocket video game, and the bleeps and beeps were driving her batty.

Thunder rolled off in the distance, and lightning flashed to the northeast. The center of the storm was still offshore, not that it mattered. She was disorganized, and most of her fury, which was north and west, would probably hit the coast. Clair believed they would outrun it as they drove to the north and toward Bar Harbor. The forecast was for Delilah to slow and stall before turning sharply out to sea. The children weighed on her mind as Clarissa pushed forward into the night.

"Bill, I'm not staying in this house tonight," Cathy said adamantly. The rain had begun to lash against the windows.

"I agree. I'm not comfortable with what has happened myself." Bill admitted. "And we have a storm hitting us as we speak."

Doug refilled their coffee cups, sat down at the kitchen bar, and said, "So, what do we do? Jump in the pickup and head to a motel?"

"No. That is not a promising idea. Not with this shit coming in. But I agree staying here in the manor is not safe either."

"So, we are caught between a storm and an evil demon?" Doug asked, taking a sip. "Really?" It was incomprehensible to him.

"How about Gaea's guest house?" Cathy suggested. "That building is new."

"I've been giving that some thought," Bill said.

Doug looked at them questioningly. "Guest house? Where is that?"

"More like an apartment, Doug. We just call it the guest house, and it's clean and ready. I had the garage rebuilt after the, well, the incident. A second story was suggested by the contractor, and I figured, why not? It just hasn't been used. There is no need for all the room we have here in the manor. There is even food in the fridge. I thought Jack and Jeremy might want to stay up there, so I had the maid service stock it. Two bedrooms and a bath and a half plus a nice living room. It's quite cozy."

The sound of thunder shook the manor causing Cathy to stand. "What are we waiting for? Let's get out of here, please. Before this crap hits or that thing comes back."

"I agree," Doug said, grabbing a bottle of scotch and running for the front door.

Bill pulled his wife behind him holding her hand. "This is not good!" The wind had picked up quickly, and rain blew in constant sheets across the courtyard. Thunder cracked, and lightning lit up the sky and the treetops surrounding the estate. Cathy screamed.

"Dammit," Bill yelled into the gale. "Run!"

Water was already starting to pool in patches on the grass, causing minor flooding. Dirt eroded from the driveway's edges, and streams of muddy water formed, threatening to become a river as it descended the steep drive toward the street below. The three sprinted toward the garage a hundred yards away. Bill slipped and fell face-first onto the mud and water covering his face and body. Cathy fell over him and quickly stood up, pulling her husband back to his feet.

To their relief, Clair had left the door open, and they stumbled into the garage and out of the rain. Bill punched a remote mounted to the wall, and the door slid toward the floor. As it hit the concrete with a heavy thud, the power went out, leaving them in total darkness and blind.

"Shit," Doug whispered.

The Archaean Horizon held her course as large waves crashed over her bow. The sea was building, and her skipper stood at the helm as precious minutes passed. Somewhere through the blinding rain, two tugboats were making their way to the sea and hopefully would be waiting at the entrance to Portland Harbor. Below decks, Tarpon struggled with his colleagues and staff to keep their precious artifacts secured. Above them, in the crew's mess, he could hear tables and chairs as they slid and crashed against bulkheads as the Horizon rolled with the swells.

"Lock that case down!" Dr. Roland Brambilla yelled across the lab.

The research vessel had been refitted for rough weather, and normally, her stabilizers would handle high seas easily. With a prop down, she was partially crippled, and the prospect of losing their priceless cargo to the bottom of the Gulf of Maine from whence it came terrified the researchers. "Check the Constance anchor!" Van Buren yelled to an intern. She nodded and stumbled out into the ship's passageway, the rocking of the ship making it difficult to walk as she made her way down to Lab 3, cold salt water lapped at her heels.

"Hold on a moment," Bill said, clutching his wife. He felt Doug's hand on his shoulder. A loud motor started, then calmed, followed by a hum. The lights flickered on, filling the garage. "Generator. Thank heavens it works."

An open stairwell built into the wall led them up to a landing constructed of pine boards and plywood. A simple door stood in the way, and Bill opened it easily. "We don't keep it locked." He said, reaching in and turning on the lights. The trio entered a living room with an open kitchen. A hallway disappeared into partial darkness before them, lit only by lightning flashing outside a few windows. Thunder shook the structure as sheets of rain splashed the windows.

"Cathy, you and Doug check the kitchen and see what we have for food. I'm going to open the rest of the apartment, turn on the lights, and check out the bedrooms. Hopefully, the maid service did its job. We need to sleep somewhere."

"I'm not sure I can sleep," Cathy stated. Bill nodded and walked toward the hall.

Doug smiled and opened a cupboard. Clean dishes were stacked neatly on the bottom shelf, with cups and glasses above them. The next door was stuffed with various canned goods: soups, vegetables, and peaches. He pulled a can off the shelf and showed it to her. "We have Spam." He announced. She laughed, opening the refrigerator. It was full as well. Cold cuts, milk, and bottles of water, as well as cheeses, eggs, bagels, and cream cheese, filled its upper half. The freezer below had frozen steaks, popsicles, ice cream and a plastic tray of ice.

"Looks like we are good here as well," Cathy confirmed. "We could outlast a blizzard."

"What about bread?"

Cathy opened another cupboard door and stood back. It was full of various loaves. Sourdough, rye, whole wheat, and a loaf of Wonder Bread made up a portion of them. "I think we can put this one back." She said, placing the white bread back into the cabinet.

"Why? I love fried Spam on Wonder Bread with a slice of melted Velveeta. Don't you?"

"Gross. There is something seriously wrong with you." Cathy said, making a face at the thought. Doug shrugged.

Bill had turned on the light down the hall and opened the guest bathroom door. It was perfectly clean, with towels hung neatly on racks. White with tiny pink lobsters woven into them. The adjoining guest bedroom proved to be the same, and he walked in and sat on the bed. Another towel lay neatly folded at the foot, along with a spare blanket. A crack of thunder followed by a flash of lightning lit up the window above the head of the bed. The entire apartment was not that large. A five-car garage was only so big, but it was ample space for two bedrooms and a couple of baths. Bill stood up and walked toward the master bedroom. He reached for the doorknob when his wife called.

"Honey, It's Clarissa on the phone. They are at Bob's."

He hadn't heard her phone ring but immediately ran toward the living room. "Are they okay?"

"Yeah. Here." Cathy said, handing him the phone.

Bill took her phone and sat on the sofa. "Baby?"

"Daddy!" Gaea said happily.

"I am so happy you are OK. And Vicky?" He heard her shriek in the background.

"She is great. I want to come home."

"Honey, the storm is bad down here. Please take care of Vicky and listen to Uncle Bob, alright?" He winced at the use of the word "uncle." The phone crackled, and Bob Pepper came on the line.

"Bill? How are you folks doing down there? Looks like you are getting the brunt of this."

"So far so good. We are holding up in the apartment over the garage."

"Why? That manor is solid as El Capitan."

"Long story, but it is what it is for the moment. We have food and water, and the genny is kicking, so we are doing fine." Bill assured him.

"I wish you all were up here with us. The weather is nice."

"Bob, it's okay if the girls are fine. Jack and Jeremy?"

"Fine, fine. They are upstairs somewhere sleeping."

Bill choked back a laugh. "Hey, Bob?"

"Yeah?"

"Doug is next to me, re-enacting the River Dance. Seems his phone is dead as well. Is Clair with you?"

"You bet. Let me put her on."

"Very funny," Doug said, taking the phone from Bill as he walked to the far corner of the room.

Cathy had wandered off, walking down the hallway as the two men talked. She glanced into the rooms that Bill had opened and approached the closed door at the end of the hall that led to the master bedroom. She grasped the knob and turned it.

"Hard to starboard!" The captain of the Archean Horizon shouted. The crippled ship turned slowly into the gale. Her crew struggled and held to their stations as blinding rain, driven by wind, flowed in sheets across the glass windows of the bridge. Other than a flash of lightning that lit up the white crests of the tempest, the floodlights on her deck did little to illuminate anything. The researchers held on within the ship's bowels as the Horizon rocked violently. Brambilla, Tarpon, and Van Buren held on to the stainless-steel tables welded to the deck.

"This is not acceptable," Mary said. "The thing I fear more than flying is drowning at sea."

"We will be fine, Mary. We have a good ship and crew, and Captain Lars knows the Archaean Horizon inside and out."

"Then why is there water on the floor?"

Gaea was nervous. She sat with Piddles looking out at the Ocean, watching the waves roll calmly in before crashing violently upon the rocks below. Something wasn't right, and she could sense it. She didn't know what she felt precisely; it was just a feeling of ill that made her sick to her stomach. She was afraid for her parents.

Vicky had retreated downstairs and was enjoying herself with Dorothy. It was the first time that she had the opportunity to be involved in a baking project. Her mother had died when she was very young, and her father had not been a cook. Opening a can of soup and turning on the stove was the limit of his culinary capabilities. When the woman invited her to help with a batch of soft molasses cookies, she was delighted to be in the kitchen and learning something new.

"Gaea says that I should always learn something new every day."

"And she is correct. That is wise advice. Please take that wooden spoon and mix this all up until it is creamy like peanut butter. The smooth kind, mind you; the batter cannot be lumpy." Dottie directed Vicky lovingly.

"Yes, Nana," Vicky said, turning the cookie dough in the bowl.

Dottie looked at the young girl. The comment had taken her aback. She had never had children, let alone grandchildren. Yet, this young girl was referring to her as her grandmother. She had been filled in by her husband on the plight of the child and the abuse she had suffered. How anyone could sustain such neglect was beyond comprehension. Yet, this girl had, and now had, a second chance at life. The Penders had picked up the responsibility with a passion and soon she would be Vicky Pender. There was no doubt concerning that outcome. Just the time that the State of Maine required prior to formal adoption stood in the way.

"You called me Nana."

"I know. I never met my own grandmother. I only had my dad, and he was mean. "

"Come here, honey, and hug me," Dottie said, opening her arms to Vicky. "You can call me Nana anytime you like."

"I like it here," Vicky said, smiling as she stepped into the embrace.

"It seems that our batter likes my apron as well." The girl's hands were covered, and most of them ended up on Dottie's apron.

"Oops."

"Don't worry, my darling. It will wash. Now, let's get these cookies into the oven, and then, you can lick the bowl."

"Yay!" The girls said in unison.

Cathy opened the door revealing a dark room. She reached in, her hand running over the wall, searching for a light switch. A cold hand grasped her wrist tightly, causing her to scream. "Cathy." A voice called, no more than a whisper. She fell back, hitting the hallway wall, and collapsed onto the floor. Lightning lit up the room. A tall woman stood in a tattered emerald dress on the far side of the bedroom. She was bloodied, her red hair matted on a fractured skull. She held the hand of a young girl. "Rebecca. Home." The corpse croaked, and the room went dark. Cathy climbed to her feet and ran to the living room, crashing into her husband.

"Bill." She stammered, clutching him and sobbing. "Tracy..."

"I got it, Bill," Doug said, running around the couple and charging down the hall.

"It was Tracy, and I...I think, Rebecca. They looked so awful."

Bill didn't even think about what his wife had seen. He had been involved in too many things to question the paranormal. If Cathy saw them in the bedroom, they were there.

CHAPTER 26
Save Us

The Archean Horizon rocked violently in the storm. Meteorologists had been proven correct as the subtropical storm intensified. Heavy rain and wind lashed the decks, setting them awash with salt water that escaped through her scuppers and poured back into the ocean.

"I've never seen such a gale this far north!" The first said over the din. The captain held the ship as steady as possible with an engine down. The Horizon climbed another steep wave before the water disappeared from beneath her hull sending the vessel crashing back into the water. Below, the scientists huddled together in a lab and held on for dear life.

The crew had done an exceptional job securing the artifacts, and so far, they held fast in their containments. Until one of the deck logs fell near the trio, still sealed in its acid-free bag.

"Dammit!" Brambilla shouted. "A cabinet has come loose. Grab that book!"

As Tarpon leaped out, the ship caught another rouge wave, causing it to shift violently, sending him crashing into a stainless-steel table, striking his head on one of the legs. The scientist collapsed onto the deck, unconscious, blood trickling from his head. Van Buren collected the artifact as Roli pulled the limp body of Tarpon to him. He cradled the doctor in his arms and examined the wound. "It's not deep." He observed aloud. "Superficial, but I am concerned about a concussion."

"There is nothing we can do in this mess," Brambilla added. "Let us hope our good captain will get us to a safe haven soon."

The look on Mary's face was not one of confidence.

On the bridge, the captain looked at his executive officer. "Send a message to the Coast Guard, please. Just to be sure. I'm not losing anyone on this day, including my ship."

"Aye."

After reviewing the available weather reports and checking Doppler radar, the harbor master of the Port of Portland made the decision to send two additional tugs to the harbor's entrance to assist the crippled Archean Horizon. The ship was a large one, and with the storm, bringing her in would be tricky. Still, he had confidence in the seamanship of his captains and their ability to handle such seagoing emergencies. Nevertheless, he gave specific orders to hold short of the ocean in relatively calmer waters behind the seawall until the Horizon neared the coast.

Gaea's mind was in turmoil. Closing her eyes, images flashed of rain and black water and of a ship being tossed and turned, struggling through the heavy seas. A beam of light pierced the darkness but provided little guidance as it skipped across the turbulent waters. She could see an old man standing at a ship's helm. A moment later, the image was replaced by another man on what appeared to be a much older ship, clutching a wooden wheel. Gaea could make out the dark eyes and black hair of the second man.

She shook her head, and she saw her parents huddling in a corner of a room illuminated by lightning strikes. A woman in a long green dress stood facing them, her right hand holding the hand of a young girl, her left arm outstretched towards them. Both apparitions looked as if they had just crawled from the grave, flesh peeling from their bodies, dried blood matting the older woman's red hair. "Rebecca, the woman croaked.

"Anubis," Gaea screamed and opened her eyes.

"Just a waking dream." She whispered to herself, breathing deeply. She had recognized Tracy and Rebecca, but it still terrified her to see them that way. Seagulls screeched outside the window and dove through clear skies grasping at crabs on the rocks below with sharp beaks. A light cool breeze tossed her hair gently. Piddles opened her eyes and yawned, stuffing her head back into the crook of Gaea's elbow. The girl cried. She knew it was not a dream.

"Full on the engine!" The Archaean Horizon's skipper yelled. "The port is just ahead, and I can see the lights of the tugs!"

"Full aye!" A voice responded. Another wave crashed across the ship's starboard side nearly sending the bridge crew to the deck as the Horizon turned and rolled.

"Captain! Look at this!" The first cried out.

"Take the helm and hold her steady." He said to a young man. As he was replaced at the ship's wheel, the skipper crossed the deck and looked at the Doppler radar. "I'll be damned. A tropical storm?"

"It looks like it and not a weak one. The eye of this thing is about to pass over us." Hilton indicated as she pointed to the center of the storm.

"Mother ocean, you bitch." Captain Enstrom muttered.

"Orders?"

"I think you know what to do."

She nodded and began to bark at the crew. "Get ready for the tugs. I want deckhands available to man the lines when ready. Get on the horn to the port master and let them know our current situation. Make certain the bilges are pumping as hard as they can. I want a damage report ASAP. Contact the Coast Guard. I want them here." The first ordered sternly. Hilton took a deep breath and followed up with a bellow: "Inform them we need a cutter and a rescue helicopter on standby. We are not about to lose the Horizon in the channel of the Port of Portland. Not on my watch! Now people. Move!"

Captain Lars Enstrom smiled and leaned back against the bulkhead, watching his first officer take command. As the crew scrambled to carry out the tasks at hand, he sighed deeply and took his hat off. Reaching into his lapel, he pulled out a handkerchief and wiped his brow. He was too old for this shit.

Gaea stood in the doorway, looking at the two boys. Normally asleep, they were clutching one another, and Jack looked terrified.

"You know, don't you?" She asked.

"He's been like this for hours and won't talk to me," Jeremy answered.

"Jack," Gaea stated. "Snap out of it. You know what is happening."

Jack blinked and looked at Jeremy, then up at her and nodded. "I am terrified of that house."

"What house?" Jer asked. "The Pender's place?"

"I knew it before we left New York. I have a feeling for things." Jack said.

"So do I." Gaea iterated. "And you know that also, don't you?"

Jack leaned into Jeremy and stared at the floor. "I've been terrified since I was a child. I see so many things and a lot are very evil. I take the visions and the dreams and write them into stories. It's my escape from the real world, and it makes me feel better."

"So, you knew about the statue," Gaea demanded. "And you didn't say anything? That is so unfair."

"I was so afraid. I didn't know what it was at first. Just a feeling that gnawed at my stomach. I would not have come to Maine, but being a writer has always been my biggest dream. Meeting your dad was something I had to do."

Gaea crossed her arms and glared at Jack. "You have the gift as well. You can see things in your dreams and sometimes when you are awake. Can't you?" She asked.

"I don't know."

"You are sensitive, and maybe more than that. We see things, feel things, and sometimes are terrified by what happens around us. You knew this when you saw that thing in the manor." Gaea informed Jack.

"I did."

"But you haven't seen Tracy or Rebecca."

"No." He replied.

"But you have felt their presence." She continued.

"Yes. And Rebecca attacked Vicky."

"You know that is not true. The statue possessed the cat, and it was he who attacked her." Gaea was adamant in her defense of Chimer and steadfast in her belief that Rebecca had not harmed Vicky.

"Then why did Vicky see Rebecca?" Jeremy inquired.

"Demons are deceitful and will use whatever means to terrify the living," Jack said, letting out the breath he didn't know he had been holding.

Gaea looked up at the ceiling. "So, what do we do?"

"We need to get back to Cape Neddick. The demon created that storm, and I believe it won't last, but your parents and Doug are in danger. The statue must be destroyed, " Jack said. He felt uncomfortable with this sudden intuition, but he trusted it.

It didn't take much convincing for Clarissa to agree to head back to Cape Neddick. Storm or no storm, her husband, Bill, and Cathy were in grave danger. Her thoughts concerning the paranormal matched Doug's, and she also believed strongly in the abilities of sensitives and mediums. She was convinced that both Jack and Gaea had such abilities. Jack was adamant that he and the girl must return to Shaw Manor and help deal with the situation. Being ten years old was of no concern. Gaea's mental abilities were needed, not her physical strength.

Bob Pepper, however, was not convinced and put up a furious argument against such a choice, calling it foolish and ill-thought-out. "You are going to take these children back into the teeth of a storm?" He fumed. "They are babies, for crying out loud!"

"Jack and Gaea are needed for the trouble back on the Cape," Clarissa argued as the two went head-to-head in Bob's office, out of earshot of the others.

"You all just got here, for Christ's sake," Bob said. "There is no need for Jeremy or Vicky to go. That would be foolishness."

"I agree, but I don't think Jeremy will part from Jack that easily. Especially if he knows that Jack could be in danger. Vicky, however, seems to have taken to your wife. I think with some help from Dorothy, she can be convinced to stay here. The girl is hardheaded."

"I will talk to her." Dorothy interrupted, walking into the room. She had been listening from the other side of the office door. A skill she had perfected over the years working for Pepper & Pepper Publishing. There were certain things a secretary needed to know, even if her boss didn't want her to know them.

"Dottie! You were eavesdropping." Bob exclaimed.

"Of course, I was. Now hush. I don't know how much I believe in all this, if any. Ghosts, demons, and hauntings. It sounds like rubbish to me. But what do I know? I am just a simple woman. I do know that no child should be put into danger of any kind, and this storm is dangerous. I have no say in this one way or the other, but I will do my best to convince Vicky to stay here. She likes to bake and be with me in the kitchen. Maybe I can use that as an enticement."

It was times like this that Robert Pepper craved a cigar to chew on as well as a shot of scotch. He walked to the windows of his office and gazed out at the Atlantic Ocean, pushing the craving from his mind. He opened one of the doors and breathed in the fresh salty air. "My bestselling author is in the middle of this, and now I have a new upcoming star that wants to go save him." Sighing deeply, the editor turned and faced Clarissa and his wife.

"Bob, the decision has already been made. I'm leaving shortly with Gaea and Jack. This debate is about Jeremy and Vicky."

"I will go and talk to the girl now," Dorothy said as she turned and left, closing the door quietly behind her.

"How can I help?" Pepper asked resignedly.

Clarissa hugged him. "Maybe an escort?"

"Police? I haven't lived here long."

"Name drop. If Bill Pender is mentioned, I think you will get some response, " she suggested.

"Go pack things up, and let me make a phone call."

"You are the best," Clarissa said, kissing him on the cheek before scurrying out the door.

He picked up the phone and called 911.

Vicky had been stubborn until Gaea had stepped in and put her friend in her place. Under no circumstances would she go back to the cape in a storm. She would stay at the Pepper mansion and "take care" of her new grandparents. The ploy worked, and Vicky gave in. Jeremy was another matter. They all stood outside of the mansion as Jack, Clarissa, and Gaea prepared to leave. "I am not staying here while you drive into a storm! Who will protect you?" Jeremy stated glaring at Jack, attempting to make him stay.

"Jer, you must, and I can take care of myself. My love, I am here to protect you. Don't you know that by now? It's been you all along."

Jeremy looked down at his feet. "I'm strong." He whispered.

"You are. You are my pillar of strength. But this is for me to do. I need you here to be with Vicky." Jack pulled Jeremy's head up with his hand and looked into his eyes. "Please." Jeremy nodded as a large SUV pulled up the drive. A quick chirp of a siren announced the arrival of the Bar Harbor police. A woman jumped out of the driver's seat and approached. The stars on her lapel denoted that she was of high rank in the department. "Mr. Pepper, I presume?" She asked, grasping his hand.

"Yes. And you are?"

"Elizabeth Milton, chief of police for the city of Bar Harbor. I understand we have a problem?"

"We need an escort down to Cape Neddick. We have friends that might be in some trouble." Clarissa said.

"Why not call the police in York County?"

"We believe it is not a police issue," Dorothy said.

"I understand it involves one Bill Pender?"

"It does," Bob answered.

"There will be no escort. Take your belongings and put them into my SUV. I am driving you. This Jeep was custom-made for foul weather. Besides, I would love to meet my favorite author," Milton instructed.

Bob forced a smile. "Thank you, chief. There is a child going with you."

Milton looked at Gaea and smiled. "She will be safe. But we need to get on the road."

Jack and Jeremy pulled the sparse bags from Cathy's Range Rover and placed them into the police vehicle. After a few hugs and promises, Bob, Jeremy, Dorothy, and Vicky watched as blue lights lit up and the SUV sped off down the drive.

CHAPTER 27
Re-Gathering

The trio had spent hours in the apartment as the storm raged outside, having stalled just on the coast. The full-bodied apparition of Tracy had shaken Cathy to her core. The dead child only added to her fear. Bill had hung on to his trembling wife as Doug returned to the living room. They talked late into the night.

"There was nothing there." Doug reiterated.

"I know what I saw. It was my best friend and a little girl." Cathy said softly. "Tracy said Rebecca and the word home."

"I'm not doubting you," Doug replied. "What does that mean? Rebecca and home?" He pondered aloud. "Perhaps the girl wants to go home and can't?"

"I can't imagine. A little girl lost for so long, just wandering through an old house, maybe searching for her mother." Tears formed in Cathy's eyes again. Lightning flashed followed immediately by a loud clap of thunder, and a crash upon the roof.

"What the hell was that?" Doug exclaimed, running to the window.

Bill ran to the opposite side of the room and looked out. "There is a tree that fell against the side of the building. Thankfully not an exceptionally large one. Hopefully, no damage."

"What the..." Doug said as he looked through the rain. "Bill, there is a police car coming up the driveway." Bill and Cathy joined him at the window and watched as the SUV pulled to a stop, its headlights and emergency flood lights setting the side of the garage awash; its blue pursuit lights spinning and flashing around the property. A policewoman stepped out into the heavy rain and wind and opened the rear door. Clarissa jumped out, followed by Jack and Gaea.

"I'm going to kill her," Doug said, heading for the stairwell.

Bill followed. "If you don't, I will."

Cathy waited at the top of the stairs as the two men opened the garage door and went to assist, her hand covering her mouth in worry.

"What are you doing here?" Doug yelled through the howling wind.

"Long story! Let's get inside!" Clair answered as loudly as she could.

Bill grabbed his daughter by the hand and rushed towards the garage's safety. Clarissa and Jack followed. The police officer quickly shut down her SUV and rushed after them. Once inside, Doug pressed the door control, and it slowly closed, shutting the weather outside.

Finally, upstairs, Cathy handed out towels before checking her daughter for injuries. Finding none, she turned to Clarissa in anger. "How dare you put my daughter in danger?" She demanded.

"Hold on, babe. There must be a good reason for this." Bill said, standing between his wife and Clarissa.

"I'll scratch her eyes out." Cathy fumed.

"We are all in danger," Jack said.

"Mom, he's right. It's not Clarissa's fault. Me and Jack made her bring us."

"But why, baby?" Her father asked.

"Anubis," Gaea said.

"What is Anubis?" The policewoman asked. "It might be none of my business, but when I hear danger, it kind of sends up a red flag. I am a cop."

"A very evil statue, and I don't think that gun on your side will help us," Jack said, walking to the kitchen. "Any hot cocoa in here?"

"Cabinet over the stove," Cathy said sharply.

"I think coffee is in order as well," Doug said. "I'll make a fresh pot."

Bill walked to the policewoman and extended his hand. "Bill Pender. Thank you for delivering my daughter and friends safely."

"You are very welcome. I am overjoyed to meet my favorite author." Bill rolled his eyes. She held up her open palms. "I won't ask for an autograph, trust me."

"If you can help sort this mess, I'll give you a signed copy of every book I have written," Pender admitted.

"Let's start sorting then, shall we? It's what I do."

Vicky was happily distracted by Dorothy Pepper, helping her with the laundry and cooking in the kitchen. Jeremy was a complete basket case. He kept looking at his watch and paced the long hallways of the mansion, occasionally going out onto a balcony to look at the ocean. The TV in the great room was set on the Weather Channel and had become another frequent stop in his endless pacing. He had tried to talk to Bob Pepper, but that did not go well. It seemed that he was more nervous than Jeremy was, and being barked at by the burley old bear did not help his frayed nerves.

Finding that Jack had forgotten his cell phone on the side table in their bedroom had nearly caused him a full mental breakdown. He tried numerous times to call Clarissa with no luck. The storm had knocked out the limited coverage that southern Maine had. The TV was reporting electric outages along the coast from Kittery to South

Portland. Jeremy clenched his fist and roared at the reporter on the screen.

Robert Pepper paced back and forth across his large office. His numerous calls to Bill, Jack and even Clarissa were dropping every time he tried. He was beginning to doubt his decision to relent on letting them leave and drive through the storm back to Cape Neddick. Having a police officer drive them was becoming little solace. He was stuck in a vacuum of doubt, with no way to confirm nor deny the suspicions that filled his mind. Ghosts and spirits were what his authors wrote about, not real life. Still, doubt was creeping into his mind. Not so much Jack, but children seemed to have a sixth sense about things. He could not fathom that Gaea would lie or make up such a story.

Bob had spent that last couple of hours researching Anubis, but all he could find was that of an Egyptian god of the underworld, and for all accounts, it did not seem evil at all. On the contrary, the beast seemed rather helpful. Anubis was the one that led the faithful to the afterlife. Not one to kill people. None of this made sense to the editor.

He sat down heavily in his chair and picked up a pen, chewing on its end. Turning on his computer, he brought up the Internet and typed in Wells Museum. A page populated the screen, and he recognized the building from when he had driven through the village. It was where Cathy had worked. Pepper scribbled down the telephone number and dialed it. A few rings later, a voice came on the line.

"Wells Maine Museum, this is Dr. Bastien, curator speaking. How can I help you?"

Bob Pepper let out a silent deep sigh. Leave it to a man such as this to be at work during a major storm. "Dr. Bastien, this Robert Pepper."

"Of course. The editor. Catherine, as well as her husband, have spoken highly of you. What do I owe the pleasure?"

"I am hoping you can help me. Can you tell me what you know about a statue you recently examined? A statue of Anubis."

"So, let me get this straight. Over in the main house, there is a possessed statue of an Egyptian god that has already killed a cat, destroyed parts of the house, and chased out two ghosts that are residents of said house; one who committed suicide, and another that is a child, and now, this thing wants the Pender's daughter?" Chief Milton said incredulously. "This is the end of April, not October 31ˢᵗ, Jack."

"That's pretty much it," Jack said, taking a sip of his hot chocolate. "But Tracy did not commit suicide. She was startled by Rebecca's sudden appearance and fell over the balcony railing."

Gaea nodded in agreement. "It's true, Mom. Rebecca didn't mean to scare her. She wanted help."

"I knew it," Cathy said softly.

"Look, if there is a threat, let me handle it. I can call in the Cape Neddick Police and we can search the house."

"That won't work," Cathy said and looked at her daughter. "I know now. You can see and feel things, can't you?" She motioned for her daughter to come to her. Gaea nodded and embraced her mother.

"My mother, your grandmother, had this gift. I never did, and I was hoping you would not be burdened with it." Cathy looked up at Jack and then at her husband. Being sensitive can be terrible to bear, and it nearly drove my mother insane at times."

"She is more than that," Jack said. "Gaea is a psychic medium and an extraordinarily strong one. More so than I am."

"What does that mean?" Bill asked.

"It means that I can see, hear, and talk with dead people. I just didn't know I could do it until that statue came on my birthday. I thought I was just having bad dreams. It's how I knew Rebecca didn't scratch Vicky 'cause she told me."

"Tracy and Rebecca are here now, aren't they?" Cathy asked.

Gaea pointed to the hallway. "Back there, and they are afraid of Anubis"

"How do you know its name?" Chief Milton asked.

"It talks to me. It wants me to be with him."

"Well, that is never going to happen!" Bill broke in on the conversation. "This is going to end right now!"

Bob Pepper hung up and scratched the stubble on his chin. "Sonofabitch." He muttered and picked up the phone again. He dialed a New York number from memory that he had not called for a very long time.

"Archdiocese New York." The voice answered. "How may the Lord assist your plight?"

CHAPTER 28
A Demon by Another Name

The storm had not waned. Wind and rain tore through the pine, maple, and oak trees that dominated the Shaw Estate, scattering broken branches and debris randomly across the grounds. The generator was doing its job providing electricity to the garage; however, the manor's lights flickered, dimming then glowing brightly before going dark. The cycle repeated itself randomly throughout the building.

"Bill," Doug said, returning to the top of the stairs, "Your house is lit up like the cop's car. I don't get it."

"It's the statue in the widow's watch," Jack said. "Whatever is possessing it is drawing power to get stronger."

"I'm sick of just sitting here. Are we going to get this, whatever it is, or not?" Chief Milton said drawing her Glock and pulling back the slide, arming the weapon.

"Stop," Gaea said loudly.

"What, baby?" Bill asked.

"You all just run over there, and you will die." She responded. "Jack." He stepped from the kitchen and walked to the girl. Sitting next to her on the couch he took her hands in his. "You know, don't you?"

"Yes." Jack stood and walked to the window, and looked out. "It is not the Egyptian myth of Anubis that we fight. Someone or some people have conjured a powerful demon that is residing in the statue. It feeds off the electricity, the storm, and the fear within us."

"That bastard," Bill said angrily. "I'm mad. No, I'm infuriated!"

"The demon feeds off anger as well," Jack said calmly, returning to the couch.

"How do we defeat it?" Cathy asked.

"The statue must be destroyed," Clarissa said. "The evil resides within it."

Jack looked up. "You are correct, but Belphegor is powerful and will not give up his prey easily."

"Prey?" Chief Milton asked.

"Gaea and myself," Jack answered. "He desires more than our bodies and souls. He craves the gifts that were given to us by God. He despises that we can see, feel, and sense the realm of the dead. We threaten his secrecy more so than any other. Gaea and I will use our ability to help defeat the monster, and together, I believe we can. Her physical presence is not needed in the house. That would be extremely dangerous. That is why Gaea must remain here, and I will go to the manor with Bill and Doug." Chief Milton cleared her throat and stood up. "And, of course, you as well, chief," Jack added.

"Bet your ass I am going." She stated.

"Vicky," Gaea said quietly.

"She would have been taken. It is good she is with Jeremy." Jack responded.

"Gaea stays here. I agree wholeheartedly with that, but who the hell is Belphegor?" Bill asked.

"I know of the demon." Doug said, pacing the floor in thought, "He is one of the seven princes of hell and is often associated with orgies and sexual debauchery. He loves children, and it doesn't matter if they are male or female. He exists for sex and the ruin of the young. I spent a year in college studying Christian methodology. I was considering becoming a priest."

"What?" Clarissa exclaimed.

"Considered, my love. I did not pursue it." Doug assured her.

"I don't give a damn if this thing is Woody the flipping woodpecker. I want it gone!" Bill yelled. "It is not getting my daughter!"

Bob Pepper sat in the great room along with his wife, Jeremy, and Vicky. The storm had reached up to Bar Harbor, and its outer bands were sending squalls ashore, lashing the mansion with heavy rain. "I thought these blasted things were supposed to get weaker as they came ashore?" He said, standing and walking to the window. "We were not even supposed to get it up here. Damn, weather people."

Dottie stood and joined her husband, hugging him from behind. "It's not their fault." She said calmingly.

"I know. I'm just worried for…well for all of them. Damn, communications blackout."

Vicky had curled up with Jeremy and was stroking her doll's hair, humming quietly.

"Honey," Dorothy asked, "if this storm upsets you, what are you going to do this winter if a blizzard comes?"

Lightning flashed, followed by a very loud clap of thunder, and the house went dark. Vicky shrieked.

"Have a generator installed," Bob replied.

Jack and Gaea had spent nearly an hour in the master bedroom with the door closed before returning to the living room. She sat down slowly, staring ahead without blinking.

"What have you done to her?" Cathy demanded.

"We have joined together in our thoughts. She is fine, but please do not disrupt the bond." Jack instructed them.

Cathy crossed her arms, clearly upset. Bill rubbed his wife's arms before hugging her. "Just keep an eye on her while I'm gone, OK?"

"Really? Really Bill? I was thinking maybe I'd go to the hairdresser." She said sarcastically.

"I'm sorry, babe. This is hard on me too."

"The demon is getting stronger," Jack said. "Let's go." Chief Milton led the way, followed by Bill, Jack, and Doug, bringing up the rear as they walked down the stairs and into the garage.

"It's still nasty out there, and it's going to be slippery. There could be debris flying in all directions, so watch yourselves." Milton said. Bill pressed the remote, and the garage door slowly opened to a fierce gale. "Dammit all." She exclaimed. The police SUV had a large branch embedded through the windshield. "That is going to cost me. This has been an unauthorized trip."

"Look," Bill said, "I'll pay for the damned windshield. Help me save my daughter."

She nodded. "That is the front door?"

"Yes," Bill said.

"OK, we go one at a time. We don't need another tree taking us all out. I will signal when the next crosses. Agreed?"

"Maybe I should go first," Bill suggested.

The chief frowned at his remark. "This is no time to be sexist, Mr. Pender. I have trained for this." Bill shrugged, and the three men nodded their accents. The distance from the garage to the front porch of the manor was no more than a hundred feet, but the weather made the short jaunt treacherous. Milton pushed forward into the gale, trying to shield her face from the stinging rain that blew from the north to the south. She managed to keep her footing, and a minute later, she stumbled up the steps and opened the front door. "We're good!" She screamed from across the drive. "C'mon!"

Bill braced himself and stepped out into the storm. A piece of debris flew at him, and he barely avoided it by stepping back into the garage.

"Shit."

"You're clear now! Come!" Milton yelled.

On Bill's second attempt he slipped and fell in the muddy water that flowed in torrents down the driveway. Picking himself up, he made it across safely and joined the police chief. Jack and Doug followed without incident, and they all stood in the foyer, breathing heavily. "Now what?" The chief asked.

"Upstairs to the widow's watch," Bill replied.

"Widow's watch? Nice name Bill." She said.

"I didn't pick the name."

"You see," Doug began, "Sea captains built such spaces..."

"Doug shut it." Bill interrupted. "We don't need a history lesson right now."

"Sorry."

"We go up the grand staircase, then directly ahead is the master bedroom," Bill explained. "On the north side of the room is a wrought iron spiral staircase that leads up to the watch and the statue."

Chief Milton pulled her pistol, checked the magazine, and cocked it. "Follow me." Jack grabbed the police officer's arm gently. "I must be the one to go first. Trust me on this. Your gun will be of no use. The demon will be focused on me." She relented reluctantly and let Jack pass but held Bill back. "I'm taking his six. Got it?"

"Yes, ma'am."

"Don't mess with a Marine," Milton said winking at Bill, continuing after Jack. Bill looked over his shoulder at Doug, who cocked his head and shrugged.

Approaching the bedroom, Jack reached for the doorknob. Milton blocked him for a moment and put her ear to the door. "All I hear is the wind outside. I can't make out anything else." She told him. Jack turned the knob and pushed the heavy door open. Inside, the room was calm and intact. The bed was made, and nothing was out of place. Jack pointed to the top of the stairs. A dull red light pulsed, turning the black iron railing to a color resembling vermilion. "Wait until I call for you," Jack said and headed for the stairs.

Cathy was close to tears. Gaea sat stoically on the sofa and stared intently at the wall. Her motherly instinct was to grab her daughter by her shoulders and shake her back into reality. No matter how intense the urge, she knew she could not. Cathy leaned forward, putting her head in her hands, and cried.

Jack climbed the stairs and disappeared into the red light. Silence followed. The wind outside subsided, and the light disappeared, replaced by darkness. Bill hung his head and sighed deeply. Chief Milton looked up and climbed the first few steps when all hell broke loose. Jack screamed.

Cathy was startled as Gaea gasped. The girl gripped the edges of the sofa so tightly that her knuckles began to turn white. Her breathing became heavier, and her face grimaced. "No, " she whispered through pursed lips.

Chief Milton charged up the remaining few steps and dropped to the landing floor. Jack hung two feet off the floor spread eagle against the bookcase behind Bill's desk. His eyes were wide and pure white. The French doors were wide open, and a black statue that looked like a dog sat, its eyes pulsing blood red. She came to her knees and took aim at the artifact. Before she could pull the trigger, the gun flew from her hands and clattered to the other side of the library.

Standing up, she was taken and thrown after the weapon, crashing against the wall and slumping to the floor unconscious.

"Shit," Bill said to Doug, peeking into the room from just below the top step.

"What do we do now?" Doug asked.

"OK," Bill said, taking a deep breath. "You go for Jack and try to help him. I will go for the statue. Maybe I can get ahold of it and toss it over the railing."

"Risky."

"Do we have a choice?"

A guttural growl came from Gaea. Her head threw back and she screamed.

A black four-door SUV made its way up the drive through the storm, fighting against the deluge of water that threatened to force it off the road and into the trees that formed the boundary of the Shaw Estate. The four-wheel drive of the vehicle held it true, and it came to a stop near the front porch of the manor. A rear window came down, and a gray-haired man looked to the tower of the manor. Red light glowed, illuminating the surrounding trees, and a scream pierced through the wind.

"What is it, Monsignor Dominic?" Sister Donovan asked.

"There is ill will here." Father Chastain said. "Something is not right."

"I have been here before and blessed this home. It had oddness about it a decade ago. This is different."

"It is an evil presence," Chastain said.

Robert Pepper's call to the Archdiocese of New York had not fallen upon deaf ears. Money talked, especially when it came to the Catholic Church. It took less than five hours for the senior cardinal of New England to be dispatched, and he was not alone. His confident Mary Eva Donovan and a Vatican-approved exorcist were dispatched with him from Boston, Massachusetts. Unbeknownst to most within the clergy, Father Chastain was also a sensitive with a degree in parapsychology prior to his joining the church. There was a need for this particular education, which he surmised prior to taking his vows, and it had served him well. "We must prepare quickly. There is no time to lose. There is danger here." Chastain reiterated. "Sister, go to there." He pointed to the garage. "But leave the girl alone." She nodded and made her way toward the building. The two priests held onto their fedoras and pushed through the storm toward the manor's front door.

"Now!" Bill yelled. Doug jumped over him and charged toward Jack. Bill stood and rushed the statue of Anubis, wrapping his arms around it. As he closed his arms around the artifact, he could feel heat radiating from the black onyx. A feeling of dread flowed through his body.

Sister Donovan made her way up to the second story of the garage and was met with a horrific sight. Cathy was on the floor rocking back and forth, her head in her hands, crying hysterically. Gaea was prone on the couch, her hands clenched at her sides, a grimace on her face, her closed eyes seeping blood that ran down her cheeks. The nun crossed herself and ran to Cathy, pulling her into her breast. "God save us." She whispered.

Bill struggled with the statue but picked it up from the floor and raised it above his head. The heaviness of the statue was nothing like he remembered when he had brought it up to the widow's watch. Its weight was crushing, and he screamed as he turned toward the balcony. A hundred feet below, the Atlantic Ocean crashed violently against jagged rocks.

Doug had reached Jack and pulled him down to the floor. He ran his hand through the boy's hair and slapped his cheek hard. "C'mon! Snap out of it!" Jack opened his eyes and shook his head. "Where is he?" Doug pointed toward the far end of the library. Bill had fallen to his knees under the crushing weight of the demon. "There."

"No," Jack said, then screamed it again more loudly. "No!" Breaking loose from Doug, Jack charged toward the statue and leaped. Bill collapsed as Jack grasped the statue from his hands, his momentum carrying him over the railing and down into the darkness below. Bill fell to the floor and rolled onto his back, breathing heavily.

Gaea slumped and fell over on the couch. "Mamma?" she muttered. Cathy and Sister Donovan sprang to Gaea to comfort her. The nun used her habit to wipe the blood from the girl's cheeks. "Baby," Cathy cooed to her daughter, stroking her hair. I was so worried." Gaea opened her eyes. The beauty of her eyes had returned, yet they were tear-filled. "He's gone, " she said, sadness in her voice.

By the time the clergymen made their way to the widow's watch, they could only assist in helping the injured. Chief Milton was starting to come around, and Doug was helping Bill get to his feet.

"Call 911, please," Bill asked Doug.

"I know. Jack." Doug replied somberly. "I'll try if my cell phone works."

"I'll do it," Milton said as she pulled the mic from her uniform. "My radio will work."

Over the next few hours, local and state police, along with fire rescue, recovered the body of Jack and tried to make sense of the scene they were presented with. Chief Elizabeth Milton had remained mum as she had her own problems to deal with back in Bar Harbor, including why she had taken a town police vehicle through a storm halfway across the State of Maine. The final police report listed the death as an unfortunate accident due to the storm. Bill and Doug were lauded as heroes for trying to save the boy who chose foolishly to climb to the widow's watch to see the storm. Bill and Doug knew better but remained silent. The case was closed.

CHAPTER 29
Juno

The storm abated as the Archean Horizon approached the harbor entrance. The rain had abruptly stopped, and rays of sunshine appeared through the dissipating clouds. "The eye, captain?" The first asked. Enstrom returned to the Doppler radar station and studied the monitor. "Nay. Heaven saved us, it's gone. I've never seen anything like this."

"How is that possible? The weather just doesn't up and switch off like a light." Hilton said, perplexed. The skipper looked at his first and shrugged. "I have learned over my years at sea not to question God's will. Just roll with it and hope for the best." She nodded. "Get the linesmen on deck and get ready to assist the tugs." The captain ordered. "I'm going below to check on crew and cargo. I will be back on the bridge shortly. And Hilton?"

Aye, sir?"

"Admirable job during this crisis." He said, turning, and then the captain walked into the starboard passageway and down to the lower deck.

Two tugboats had gently pushed the Archaean Horizon to the largest dock in the Portland Harbor. Captain Lars Enstrom stood outside the bridge on the port weather deck, watching as deckhands scrambled with the heavy lines securing his ship to the concrete pier.

"That was a fine show of seamanship, skipper," Tarpon said, joining the captain.

The old man glanced at the doctor and smiled wryly. "I have a good crew and an exceptional first officer."

Jeff had not noticed in the past; however, it became apparent to him now just how sea-worn the captain of the Archaean Horizon had become. Wrinkles around the man's eyes had grown more prominent, and his hair had gone from gray to almost white. "You are done, aren't you?"

"I am. I will not go to sea again as the Horizon's captain. That will be up to my first." Lars confirmed.

"Why do you call her your first and not by her name?"

"Patricia? I do, but not often when at sail. I have strict professional rules as to how I address my officers and crew. Because of this, respect is gained, and you, my friend, will have a fine new captain."

Tarpon looked down at the pier and the calm water that lapped at the hull of the ship. "Where are you going?"

"I have a condominium in Key West. I will go there."

"A condo? You?" Tarpon asked in shock.

"And can you see me mowing a lawn?" Enstrom chuckled.

"I guess not. But what are your plans?"

"I've become a partner with a young fellow. I am going to skipper a 45-foot trimaran from Key West out to the reef and back for the paying tourists that want to snorkel and swim."

"You! Going back to being a pleasure boat captain? I can't believe it."

"Why not? It's day sailing and only in pleasant weather, mind you. Out early and back to dock the same day. Pretty girls lying about in swimsuits." The old man grinned.

"I'm shocked. What about the fishing?"

"Of course. The catamaran is seasonal. I have plenty of time for fishing. And for the Blind Pig Saloon."

"What is that?" Tarpon asked.

"Ah. It is a wonderful drinking establishment that has been in Key West for decades. It was the first place that Ernest Hemingway went to when he moved to the island."

"I did not know that. Perhaps I will have to come visit you, my friend." Jeff said, clapping the captain on the shoulder and feeling a sense of loss.

"Perhaps you will."

Vicky and Gaea were busy being chased around the front lawn of Shaw Manor by Piddles, who barked happily, nipping at the girl's spring dresses. With the arrival of June, the school was set to close for summer vacation. "They have missed a lot of school. You know that." Bill said, looking at his wife.

"It's not their fault. And Vicky wants to start taking piano lessons with Gaea. But no summer school for them."

"You're going to home-school them?"

"Why not? And you can help." Cathy said, smiling.

"Me? I'm not qualified. I spell cat, K A T."

"C'mon Bill. I need some help. Doug and Clarissa are buying the house down the road..."

"Which is really cool. And Jeremy is taking over a position in Pepper and Pepper to make sure that Jack's work will be published."

"What about Jeremy's shop in New York?" Cathy asked. "I'm sad I didn't have time to take him to mine."

"Clair told me that he was keeping it and is going to work both jobs."

"Wow. Oh, and thank you for agreeing to allow Jack to be buried in our cemetery. He had no family other than Jeremy."

"Bob said he would have covered all expenses for whatever services Jeremy wanted," Bill said. "He chose here. I'm going to miss that kid. He had a ton of talent."

"He saved Gaea and Rebecca," Cathy admitted somberly.

"Maybe all of us. That damned thing was nasty." Bill agreed.

"Are you sure it is gone, Bill? I don't know if I can go through another bout of this. Maybe our home is cursed."

"Nonsense, honey. How could you have known that that statue was possessed? And by a powerful demon, no less. No, this was a coincidence and nothing more." He tried to assure his wife. "Besides, the police mentioned a broken statue when they recovered Jack's body."

"What did you say about that?"

"Not much. The ocean is filled with junk that washes ashore these days. So, I don't think it matters."

Cathy sighed. "I'm glad that our girls are feeling better, " she said, watching as they ran and played on the front lawn with the puppy. I hope Jeremy is coping as well as our children."

"He is welcome whenever he wants to come. Bob and Dottie have an open invitation for him as well. And our daughters like to visit them too. Vicky calls Dottie Grandma." Bill sighed, smiled, and rocked gently in his Cape Cod rocking chair. "Having them up in Bar Harbor for the girls to go visit is great for us. Gives us time for ourselves. You know, maybe taking a vacation. I would like to fly to Greece and visit Santorini. I just hope there will be no more drama here at the manor." Bill said, taking his wife's hand.

"Bill?" Cathy said, looking at him.

"Yeah?"

"I'm pregnant with our son."

A Few Off the Old Royal:

The Widow's Watch: A Haunting on Cape Neddick (1 of 3)

The Widow's Watch: Dreamer's Hideaway (2 of 3)

Tales of the Little Lagoon: Kiwa's Story

The Dream Catcher

Spirits and Tales

One with Paper In:

The Widow's Watch: Shaw Manor (3 of 3)